W9-BSD-129

Halloween.

Sly does it. Tiptoe catspaws. Slide and creep.

But why? What for? How? Who? When! Where did it all begin?

"You don't know, do you?" asks Carapace Clavicle Moundshroud climbing out of the pile of leaves under the Halloween Tree. "You don't *really* know!"

"Well," answers Tom the Skeleton, "er—no."

Was it—

In Egypt four thousand years ago, on the anniversary of the big death of the sun?

Or a million years before that, by the night fires of the cavemen?

Or in Druid Britain at the *Ssssswooommmm* of Samhain's scythe?

Or among the witches, all across Europe—multitudes of hags, crones, magicians, demons, devils?

Or high above Paris, where strange creatures froze to stone and lit the gargoyles of Notre Dame?

Or in Mexico, in cemeteries full of candlelight and tiny candy people on *El Dia de los Muertos*—the Day of the Dead?

Or *where?*

A thousand pumpkin smiles look down from the Halloween Tree, and twice-times-a-thousand fresh-cut eyes glare and wink and blink, as Mound-shroud leads the eight trick-or-treaters—no, *nine,* But where *is* Pipkin?—on a leaf-tossed, kite-flying, gliding, broomstick-riding trip to learn the secret of All Hallows' Eve.

And they do.

"Well," asks Moundshroud at journey's end, "which was it? A Trick or a Treat?"

"Both!" all agree.

And so will you.

Bantam Spectra Books by Ray Bradbury
Ask your bookseller for the titles you have missed

THE MARTIAN CHRONICLES
SOMETHING WICKED THIS WAY COMES
DANDELION WINE
THE ILLUSTRATED MAN
THE HALLOWEEN TREE
THE TOYNBEE CONVECTOR
CLASSIC STORIES 1: THE GOLDEN APPLES OF THE SUN/R IS FOR
     ROCKET
CLASSIC STORIES 2: A MEDICINE FOR MELANCHOLY/S IS FOR SPACE

THE
HALLOWEEN
TREE

RAY BRADBURY

Illustrated by Joseph Mugnaini

BANTAM BOOKS
NEW YORK • TORONTO • LONDON • SYDNEY • AUCKLAND

*This edition contains the complete text
of the original hardcover edition.*
NOT ONE WORD HAS BEEN OMITTED.

RL 6, IL age 12 and up

THE HALLOWEEN TREE
*A Bantam Spectra Book / published by arrangement with
Alfred A. Knopf, Inc.*

PRINTING HISTORY
Knopf edition published June 1972
Bantam edition / October 1974
15 printings through May 1990

*All rights reserved.
Copyright © 1972 by Ray Bradbury.
Illustrations copyright © 1972 by Alfred A. Knopf.
Cover art copyright © 1981 by Bantam Books.
No part of this book may be reproduced or transmitted
in any form or by any means, electronic or mechanical,
including photocopying, recording, or by any information
storage and retrieval system, without permission in writing
from the publisher.
For information address: Alfred A. Knopf, Inc.,
201 E. 50th Street, New York, N.Y. 10022.*

ISBN 0-553-25823-0

Published simultaneously in the United States and Canada

*Bantam Books are published by Bantam Books, a division of Bantam
Doubleday Dell Publishing Group, Inc. Its trademark, consisting of the
words "Bantam Books" and the portrayal of a rooster, is Registered in U.S.
Patent and Trademark Office and in other countries. Marca Registrada.
Bantam Books, 666 Fifth Avenue, New York, New York 10103.*

PRINTED IN THE UNITED STATES OF AMERICA

OPM   25 24 23 22 21 20 19 18 17 16 15

With love for

MADAME MAN'HA GARREAU-DOMBASLE

met twenty-seven years

ago in the graveyard at

midnight on the Island

of Janitzio at Lake Patzcuaro,

Mexico, and remembered

on each anniversary of

The Day of the Dead.

Chapter 1

It was a small town by a small river and a small lake in a small northern part of a Midwest state. There wasn't so much wilderness around you couldn't see the town. But on the other hand there wasn't so much town you couldn't see and feel and touch and smell the wilderness. The town was full of trees. And dry grass and dead flowers now that autumn was here. And full of fences to walk on and sidewalks to skate on and a large ravine to tumble in and yell across. And the town was full of . . .

Boys.

And it was the afternoon of Halloween.

And all the houses shut against a cool wind.

And the town full of cold sunlight.

But suddenly, the day was gone.

Night came out from under each tree and spread.

1

Behind the doors of all the houses there was a scurry of mouse feet, muted cries, flickerings of light.

Behind one door, Tom Skelton, aged thirteen, stopped and listened.

The wind outside nested in each tree, prowled the sidewalks in invisible treads like unseen cats.

Tom Skelton shivered. Anyone could see that the wind was a special wind this night, and the darkness took on a special feel because it was All Hallows' Eve. Everything seemed cut from soft black velvet or gold or orange velvet. Smoke panted up out of a thousand chimneys like the plumes of funeral parades. From kitchen windows drifted two pumpkin smells: gourds being cut, pies being baked.

The cries behind the locked house doors grew more exasperated as shadows of boys flew by windows. Half-dressed boys, greasepaint on their cheeks; here a hunchback, there a medium-sized giant. Attics were still being rummaged, old locks broken, old steamer chests disemboweled for costumes.

Tom Skelton put on his bones.

He grinned at the spinal cord, the ribcage,

the kneecaps stitched white on black cotton.

Lucky! he thought. What a name you got! Tom Skelton. Great for Halloween! Everyone calls you Skeleton! So what do you wear?

Bones.

Wham. Eight front doors banged shut.

Eight boys made a series of beautiful leaps over flowerpots, rails, dead ferns, bushes, landing on their own dry-starched front lawns. Galloping, rushing, they seized a final sheet, adjusted a last mask, tugged at strange mushroom caps or wigs, shouting at the way the wind took them along, helped their running; glad of the wind, or cursing boy curses as masks fell off or hung sidewise or stuffed up their noses with a muslin smell like a dog's hot breath. Or just letting the sheer exhilaration of being alive and out on this night pull their lungs and shape their throats into a yell and a yell and a . . . yeeeellll!

Eight boys collided at one intersection.

"Here I am: Witch!"

"Apeman!"

"Skeleton!" said Tom, hilarious inside his bones.

"Gargoyle!"

"Beggar!"

"Mr. Death Himself!"

Bang! They shook back from their concussions, all happy-fouled and tangled under a street-corner light. The swaying electric lamp belled in the wind like a cathedral bell. The bricks of the street became planks of a drunken ship all tilted and foundered with dark and light.

Behind each mask was a boy.

"Who's that?" Tom Skelton pointed.

"Won't tell. Secret!" cried the Witch, disguising his voice.

Everyone laughed.

"Who's that?"

"Mummy!" cried the boy inside the ancient yellowed wrappings, like an immense cigar stalking the night streets.

"And who's—?"

"No time!" said Someone Hidden Behind Yet Another Mystery of Muslin and Paint. "Trick or treat!"

"Yeah!"

Shrieking, wailing, full of banshee mirth they ran, on everything except sidewalks, going up

4

into the air over bushes and down almost upon yipping dogs.

But in the middle of running, laughing, barking, suddenly, as if a great hand of night and wind and smelling-something-wrong stopped them, they stopped.

"Six, seven, eight."

"That *can't* be! Count again."

"Four, five, six—"

"Should be *nine* of us! Someone's missing!"

They sniffed each other, like fearful beasts.

"Pipkin's not here!"

How did they know? They were all hidden behind masks. And yet, and yet . . .

They could *feel* his absence.

"Pipkin! He's never missed a Halloween in a zillion years. Boy, this is awful. Come on!"

In one vast swerve, one doglike trot and ramble, they circled round and down the middle of the cobble-brick street, blown like leaves before a storm.

"Here's his place!"

They pulled to a halt. There was Pipkin's house, but not enough pumpkins in the windows, not enough cornshocks on the porch, not

5

enough spooks peering out through the dark glass in the high upstairs tower room.

"Gosh," said someone, "what if Pipkin's *sick?*"

"It wouldn't be Halloween without Pipkin."

"Not Halloween," they moaned.

And someone threw a crabapple at Pipkin's front door. It made a small thump, like a rabbit kicking the wood.

They waited, sad for no reason, lost for no reason. They thought of Pipkin and a Halloween that might be a rotten pumpkin with a dead candle if, if, if—Pipkin wasn't there.

Come on, Pipkin. Come out and *save* the Night!

Chapter 2

Why were they waiting, afraid for one small
boy?

Because . . .

Joe Pipkin was the greatest boy who ever
lived. The grandest boy who ever fell out of a
tree and laughed at the joke. The finest boy who
ever raced around the track, winning, and then,
seeing his friends a mile back somewhere, stum-
bled and fell, waited for them to catch up, and
joined, breast and breast, breaking the winner's
tape. The jolliest boy who ever hunted out all
the haunted houses in town, which are hard
to find, and came back to report on them and
take all the kids to ramble through the basements and scramble up the ivy outside-bricks
and shout down the chimneys and make water
off the roofs, hooting and chimpanzee-dancing
and ape-bellowing. The day Joe Pipkin was

born all the Orange Crush and Nehi soda bottles in the world fizzed over; and joyful bees
swarmed countrysides to sting maiden ladies.
On his birthdays, the lake pulled out from the
shore in midsummer and ran back with a tidal
wave of boys, a big leap of bodies and a down-
crash of laughs.

Dawns, lying in bed, you heard a birdpeck
at the window. Pipkin.

You stuck your head out into the snow-water-
clear-summer-morning air.

There in the dew on the lawn rabbit prints
showed where, just a moment ago, not a dozen
rabbits but one rabbit had circled and criss-
crossed in a glory of life and exultation, bound-
ing hedges, clipping ferns, tromping clover. It
resembled the switchyards down at the rail de-
pot. A million tracks in the grass but no . . .

Pipkin.

And here he rose up like a wild sunflower in
the garden. His great round face burned with
fresh sun. His eyes flashed Morse code signals:

"Hurry up! It's almost over!"

"What?"

"Today! Now! Six A.M.! Dive down! *Wade* in
it!"

Or: "This *summer*! Before you know, bang! —it's gone! Quick!"

And he sank away in sunflowers to come up all onions.

Pipkin, oh, dear Pipkin, finest and loveliest of boys.

How he ran so fast no one knew. His tennis shoes were ancient. They were colored green of forests jogged through, brown from old harvest trudges through September a year back, tar-stained from sprints along the docks and beaches where the coal barges came in, yellow from careless dogs, splinter-filled from climbing wood fences. His clothes were scarecrow clothes, worn by Pipkin's dogs all night, loaned to them for strolls through town, with chew marks along the cuffs and fall marks on the seat.

His hair? His hair was a great hedgehog bristle of bright brown-blond daggers sticking in all directions. His ears, pure peachfuzz. His hands, mittened with dust and the good smell of airedales and peppermint and stolen peaches from the far country orchards.

Pipkin. An assemblage of speeds, smells, textures; a cross section of all the boys who ever ran, fell, got up, and ran again.

9

No one, in all the years, had ever seen him sitting still. He was hard to remember in school, in one seat, for one hour. He was the last into the schoolhouse and the first exploded out when the bell ended the day.

Pipkin, sweet Pipkin.

Who yodeled and played the kazoo and hated girls more than all the other boys in the gang combined.

Pipkin, whose arm around your shoulder, and secret whisper of great doings this day, protected you from the world.

Pipkin.

God got up early just to see Pipkin come out of his house, like one of those people on a weatherclock. And the weather was always fine where Pipkin was.

Pipkin.

They stood in front of his house.

Any moment now that door would open wide.

Pipkin would jump out in a blast of fire and smoke.

And Halloween would REALLY begin!

Come on, Joe, oh, Pipkin, they whispered, come on!

Chapter 3

The front door opened.

Pipkin stepped out.

Not flew. Not banged. Not exploded.

Stepped out.

And came down the walk to meet his friends.

Not running. And *not* wearing a mask! No mask!

But moving along like an old man, almost.

"Pipkin!" they shouted, to scare away their uneasiness.

"Hi, gang," said Pipkin.

His face was pale. He tried to smile, but his eyes looked funny. He was holding his right side with one hand as if he had a boil there.

They all looked at his hand. He took his hand away from his side.

"Well," he said with faint enthusiasm. "We ready to go?"

"Yeah, but *you* don't look ready," said Tom. "You sick?"

"On Halloween?" said Pipkin. "You kidding?"

"Where's your costume—?"

"You go on ahead, I'll catch up."

"No, Pipkin, we'll wait for you to—"

"Go on," said Pipkin, saying it slowly, his face deathly pale now. His hand was back on his side.

"You got a stomachache?" asked Tom. "You told your folks?"

"No, no, I can't! They'd—" Tears burst from Pipkin's eyes. "It's nothing, I tell you. Look. Go straight on toward the ravine. Head for the House, okay? The place of the Haunts, yeah? Meet you there."

"You swear?"

"Swear. Wait'll you see my costume!"

The boys began to back off. On the way, they touched his elbow, or knocked him gently in the chest, or ran their knuckles along his chin in a fake fight. "Okay, Pipkin. As long as you're sure—"

12

"I'm sure." He took his hand away from his side. His face colored for a moment as if the pain were gone. "On your marks. Get set. Go!"

When Joe Pipkin said "Go," they Went.

They ran.

They ran backward halfway down the block, so they could see Pipkin standing there, waving at them.

"Hurry up, Pipkin!"

"I'll catch you!" he shouted, a long way off.

The night swallowed him.

They ran. When they looked back again, he was gone.

They banged doors, they shouted Trick or Treat and their brown paper bags began to fill with incredible sweets. They galloped with their teeth glued shut with pink gum. They ran with red wax lips bedazzling their faces.

But all the people who met them at doors looked like candy factory duplicates of their own mothers and fathers. It was like never leaving home. Too much kindness flashed from every window and every portal. What they wanted was to hear dragons belch in basements and banged castle doors.

And so, still looking back for Pipkin, they

reached the edge of town and the place where civilization fell away in darkness.

The Ravine.

The ravine, filled with varieties of night sounds, lurkings of black-ink stream and creek, lingerings of autumns that rolled over in fire and bronze and died a thousand years ago. From this deep place sprang mushroom and toadstool and cold stone frog and crawdad and spider. There was a long tunnel down there under the earth in which poisoned waters dripped and the echoes never ceased calling Come Come Come and if you do you'll stay forever, forever, drip, forever, rustle, run, rush, whisper, and never go, never go go go . . .

The boys lined up on the rim of darkness, looking down.

And then Tom Skelton, cold in his bones, whistled his breath in his teeth like the wind blowing over the bedroom screen at night. He pointed.

"Oh, hey—*that's* where Pipkin told us to go!"

He vanished.

All looked. They saw his small shape race down the dirt path into one hundred million tons of night all crammed in that huge dark

14

pit, that dank cellar, that deliciously frightening ravine.

Yelling, they plunged after.

Where they had been was empty.

The town was left behind to suffer itself with sweetness.

Chapter 4

They ran down through the ravine at a swift rush, all laughing, jostling, all elbows and ankles, all steamy snort and roustabout, to stop in collision when Tom Skelton stopped and pointed up the path.

"There," he whispered. "There's the *only* house in town worth visiting on Halloween! There!"

"Yeah!" said everyone.

For it was true. The house was special and fine and tall and dark. There must have been a thousand windows in its sides, all shimmering with cold stars. It looked as if it had been cut out of black marble instead of built out of timbers, and inside? who could guess how many rooms, halls, breezeways, attics. Superior and inferior attics, some higher than others, some more filled with dust and webs and ancient leaves or gold buried above ground in the sky but lost away so high no ladder in town could take you there.

The house beckoned with its towers, invited with its gummed-shut doors. Pirate ships are a tonic. Ancient forts are a boon. But a house, a *haunted* house, on All Hallows' Eve? Eight small hearts beat up an absolute storm of glory and approbation.

"Come on."

But they were already crowding up the path. Until they stood at last by a crumbling wall, looking up and up and still farther up at the great tombyard top of the old house. For that's what it seemed. The high mountain peak of the mansion was littered with what looked like black bones or iron rods, and enough chimneys to choke out smoke signals from three dozen fires on sooty hearths hidden far below in the dim bowels of this monster place. With so many chimneys, the roof seemed a vast cemetery, each chimney signifying the burial place of some old god of fire or enchantress of steam, smoke, and firefly spark. Even as they watched, a kind of bleak exhalation of soot breathed up out of some four dozen flues, darkening the sky still more, and putting out some few stars.

"Boy," said Tom Skelton, "Pipkin sure knows what he's talking about!"

"Boy," said all, agreeing.

They crept along a weed-infested path toward the crumpled front porch.

Tom Skelton, alone, itched his bony foot up on the first porch-step. The others gasped at his bravery. So, now, finally in a mob, a compact mass of sweating boys moved up on the porch amid fierce cries of the planks underfoot, and shudderings of their bodies. Each wished to pull back, swivel about, run, but found himself trapped against the boy behind or in front or to the side. So, with a pseudopod thrust out here or there, the amoebic form, the large perspiration of boys leaned and made a run and a stop to the front door of the house which was as tall as a coffin and twice as thin.

They stood there for a long moment, various hands reaching out like the legs of an immense spider as if to twist that cold knob or reach up for the knocker on that front door. Meanwhile,

19

the wooden floorings of the porch sank and wallowed beneath their weight, threatening at every shift of proportion to give way and fling them into some cockroach abyss beneath. The planks, each turned to an A or an F or a C, sang out their uncanny music as heavy shoes scraped on them. And if there had been time and it were noon, they might have danced out a cadaver's tune or a skeleton's rigadoon, for who can resist an ancient porch which, like a gigantic xylophone, only wants to be jumped on to make music?

But they were not thinking this.

Henry-Hank Smith (for that's who it was), hidden inside his black Witch's costume, cried: "Look!"

And all looked at the knocker on the door. Tom's hand trembled out to touch it.

"A Marley knocker!"

"What?"

"You know, Scrooge and Marley, a *Christmas Carol!*" whispered Tom.

And indeed the face that made up the knocker on the door was the face of a man with a dread toothache, his jaw bandaged, his hair askew, his teeth prolapsed, his eyes wild. Dead-as-a-doornail Marley, friend to Scrooge, inhabit-er of lands beyond the grave, doomed to wander this earth forever until . . .

"Knock," said Henry-Hank.

Tom Skelton took hold of old Marley's cold and grisly jaw, lifted it, and let it fall.

All jumped at the concussion!

The entire house shook. Its bones ground together. Shades snap-furled up so that windows blinked wide their ghastly eyes.

Tom Skelton cat-leaped to the porch rail, staring up.

On the rooftop, weird weathercocks spun. Two-headed roosters whirled in the sneezed wind. A gargoyle on the western rim of the house erupted twin snorts of rain-funnel dust. And down the long snaking serpentine rain-spouts of the house, after the sneeze had died and the weathercocks ceased spinning, vagrant wisps of autumn leaf and cobweb fell gusting out onto the dark grass.

Tom whirled to look at the faintly shudder-ing windows. Moonlit reflections trembled in the glass like schools of disturbed silver minnows. Then the front door gave a shake, a twist of its knob, a grimace of its Marley knocker, and flung itself wide.

The wind made by the suddenly opening door almost knocked the boys off the porch. They seized one another's elbows, yelling.

Then the darkness within the house inhaled. A wind sucked through the gaping door. It pulled at the boys, dragging them across the porch. They had to lean back so as not to be snatched into the deep dark hall. They struggled, shouted, clutched the porch rails. But then the wind ceased.

Darkness moved within darkness.

Inside the house, a long way off, someone was walking toward the door. Whoever it was must have been dressed all in black for they could see nothing but a pale white face drifting on the air.

An evil smile came and hung in the doorway before them.

Behind the smile, the tall man hid in shadow. They could see his eyes now, small pinpoints of green fire in little charred pits of sockets, looking out at them.

"Well," said Tom. "Er—trick or treat?"

"Trick?" said the smile in the dark. "Treat?"

"Yes, sir."

The wind played a flute in a chimney somewhere; an old song about time and dark and
far places. The tall man shut up his smile like
a bright pocketknife.

"No treats," he said. "Only—*trick!*"

The door *slammed!*

The house thundered with showers of dust.

Dust puffed out the rainspout again, in fluffs,
like an emergence of downy cats.

Dust gasped from open windows. Dust snorted from the porchboards under their feet.

The boys stared at the locked shut-fast front
door. The Marley knocker was not scowling
now, but smiling an evil smile.

"What's he *mean?*" asked Tom. "No treats,
only trick?"

Backing off around the side of the house they
were astonished at the sounds it made. A whole
rigamarole of whispers, squeaks, creaks, wails,
and murmurs, and the night wind was careful to
let the boys hear them all. With every step they
took, the great house leaned after them with soft
groans.

They rounded the far side of the house and
stopped.

For there was the Tree.

And it was such a tree as they had never seen in all their lives.

It stood in the middle of a vast yard behind the terribly strange house. And this tree rose up some one hundred feet in the air, taller than the high roofs and full and round and well branched, and covered all over with rich assortments of red and brown and yellow autumn leaves.

"But," whispered Tom, "oh, look. What's up *in* that tree!"

For the Tree was hung with a variety of pumpkins of every shape and size and a number of tints and hues of smoky yellow or bright orange.

"A pumpkin tree," someone said.

"No," said Tom.

The wind blew among the high branches and tossed their bright burdens, softly.

"A Halloween Tree," said Tom.

And he was right.

Chapter 5

The pumpkins on the Tree were not mere pumpkins. Each had a face sliced in it. Each face was different. Every eye was a stranger eye. Every nose was a weirder nose. Every mouth smiled hideously in some new way.

There must have been a thousand pumpkins on this tree, hung high and on every branch. A thousand smiles. A thousand grimaces. And twice-times-a-thousand glares and winks and blinks and leerings of fresh-cut eyes.

And as the boys watched, a new thing happened.

The pumpkins began to come alive.

One by one, starting at the bottom of the Tree and the nearest pumpkins, candles took

fire within the raw interiors. This one and then
that and this and then still another, and on up
and around, three pumpkins here, seven pumpkins still higher, a dozen clustered beyond, a
hundred, five hundred, a thousand pumpkins
lit their candles, which is to say brightened up
their faces, showed fire in their square or round
or curiously slanted eyes. Flame guttered in
their toothed mouths. Sparks leaped out their
ripe-cut ears.

And from somewhere two voices, three or
maybe four voices whispered and chanted a
kind of singsong or old sea shanty of the sky and
time and the earth turning over into sleep. The
rainspouts blew spiderdust:

"It's big, it's broad . . ."

A voice smoked from the rooftop chimney:

It's broad, it's bright . . .
It fills the sky of All Hallows' Night . . ."

From open windows somewhere, cobwebs
drifted:

*"The strangest sight you've ever seen.
The Monster Tree on Halloween."*

The candles flickered and flared. The wind
crooned in, the wind crooned out the pumpkin
mouths, tuning the song:

*"The leaves have burned to gold and red
The grass is brown, the old year dead,
But hang the harvest high, Oh see!
The candle constellations on the Hallow-
een Tree"*

Tom felt his mouth stir like a small mouse,
wanting to sing:

*"The stars they turn, the candles burn
And the mouse-leaves scurry on the cold
wind bourne,
And a mob of smiles shine down on thee
From the gourds hung high on the
Halloween Tree.*

*The smile of the Witch, and the smile of
the Cat,
The smile of the Beast, the smile of the Bat,*

29

*The smile of the Reaper taking his fee
All cut and glimmer on the Halloween
   Tree . . ."*

Smoke seemed to sift from Tom's mouth:
"Halloween Tree . . ."
All the boys whispered it:
"Halloween . . . Tree . . ."
And then there was silence.
And during the silence the last of the triples and quadruples of All Hallows' Tree candles were lit in titanic constellations woven up through the black branches and peeking down through the twigs and crisp leaves.
And the Tree had now become one vast substantial Smile.
The last of the pumpkins now were lit. The air around the Tree was Indian-summer-breathing warm. The Tree exhaled sooty smoke and raw-pumpkin smell upon them.
"Gosh," said Tom Skelton.
"Hey, what kind of place is this?" asked Henry-Hank, the Witch. "I mean, first the house, that man and no treats only tricks, and now—? I never saw a tree like this in my life. Like a Christmas tree only bigger and all those

candles and pumpkins. What's it mean? What's it celebrate?"

"Celebrate! a vast voice whispered some-where, perhaps in a chimney soot bellows, or perhaps all the windows of the house opened like mouths at the same moment behind them, sliding up, sliding down, announcing the word "Celebrate!" with breathings-out of darkness. "Yes," said the gigantic whisper, which trem-bled the candles in the pumpkins. ". . . cele-bration . . ."

The boys leaped around.

But the house was still. The windows were closed and brimmed with pools of moonlight.

"Last one in's an Old Maid!" cried Tom, suddenly.

And a bon of leaves lay waiting like old fires, old gold.

And the boys ran and dived at the huge love-ly pile of autumn treasure.

And in the moment of diving, about to vanish beneath the leaves in crisp swarms, yelling, shouting, shoving, falling, there was an immense gulp of breath, a seizing in of air. The boys yelped, pulled back as if an invisible whip had struck them.

31

For coming up out of the pile of leaves was a bony white hand, all by itself.

And following it, all smiles, hidden one moment but now revealed as it slid upward, was a white skull.

And what had been a delicious pool of oak and elm and poplar leaves to thrash and sink and hide in, now became the last place on all this world the boys wanted to be. For the white bony hand was flying on the air. And the white skull rose to hover before them.

And the boys fell back, colliding, sneezing out their air in panics, until in one wild mass they fell flat upon the earth and writhed and tore at the grass to fight free, scramble, try to run.

"Help!" they cried.

"Oh, yes, help," said the Skull.

Then peal after peal of laughter froze them further as the hand upon the air, the bony skeleton hand, reached up, took hold of the white skull face and—peeled it down and off!

The boys blinked once behind their masks. Their jaws dropped, though none could see them dropping.

The huge man in dark clothes soared up out

of the leaves, taller and yet taller. He grew like a tree. He put out branches that were hands. He stood framed against the Halloween Tree itself, his outstretched arms and long white bony fingers festooned with orange globes of fire and burning smiles. His eyes were pressed tight as he roared his laughter. His mouth gaped wide to let an autumn wind rush out.

"Not treat, boys, no, not Treat! Trick, boys, Trick! *Trick!*"

They lay there waiting for the earthquake to come. And it came. The tall man's laughter took hold of the ground and gave it a shake. This tremor, passed through their bones, came out their mouths. And it came out in the form of still more laughter!

They sat up amid the ruins of the thrashed-about leaf pile, surprised. They put their hands to their masks to feel the hot air leaping out in small gusts of echoing mirth.

Then they looked up at the man as if to verify their surprise.

"Yes, boys, that, *that* was a Trick! You'd forgotten? No, you never *knew!*"

And he leaned against the Tree, finishing out

his fits of happiness, shaking the trunk, making the thousand pumpkins shiver and the fires inside to smoke and dance.

Warmed by their laughter, the boys got up to feel their bones and see if anything was broken. Nothing was. They stood in a small mob under the Halloween Tree, waiting, for they knew this was only the beginning of something new and special and grand and fine.

"Well," said Tom Skelton.

"Well, Tom," said the man.

"Tom?" cried everyone else. "Is that *you?*"

Tom, in the Skeleton mask, stiffened.

"Or is it Bob or Fred, no, no, that must be Ralph," said the man, quickly.

"All of those!" sighed Tom, clapping his mask hard in place, relieved.

"Yeah, all!" said everyone.

The man nodded, smiling. "Well now! Now you know something about Halloween you never knew before. How did you like my Trick?"

"Trick, yes, trick." The boys were catching fire with the idea. It made all the good glue go out of their joints and put a little dust of sin in their blood. They felt it stir around until it pumped on up to light their eyes and stretch their lips to show their happy-dog teeth. "Yeah, sure."

"Is this what *you* used to do on Halloween?" asked the Witch boy.

"This, and more. But, let me introduce myself! Moundshroud is the name. Carapace Clavicle Moundshroud. Does that have a ring, boys? Does it *sound* for you?"

It sounds, the boys thought, oh, oh, it *sounds* . . .!

Moundshroud.

"A fine name," said Mr. Moundshroud, giving it a full sepulchral night-church sound. "And a fine night. And all the deep dark wild long history of Halloween waiting to swallow us whole!"

"Swallow us?"

"Yes!" cried Moundshroud. "Lads, look at yourselves. Why are you, boy, wearing that Skull face? And you, boy, carrying a scythe, and you, lad, made up like a Witch? And you, you, you!" He thrust his bony finger at each mask. "You don't know, do you? You just put on those faces and old mothball clothes and jump out, but you don't *really* know, do you?"

"Well," said Tom, a mouse behind his skull-white muslin. "Er—no."

"Yeah," said the Devil boy. "Come to think of it, Why *am* I wearing this?" He fingered his red-cloak and sharp rubber horns and lovely pitchfork.

"And me, this," said the Ghost, trailing its long white graveyard sheets.

And all the boys were given to wonder, and touched their own costumes and refit their own masks.

"Then wouldn't it be fun for you to find out?" asked Mr. Moundshroud. "I'll tell you! No, I'll *show* you! If only there was time—"

"It's only six thirty. Halloween hasn't even begun!" said Tom-in-his-cold-bones.

"True!" said Mr. Moundshroud. "All right, lads—come *along!*"

He strode. They ran.

At the edge of the deep dark night ravine he pointed over the rim of the hills and the earth, away from the light of the moon, under the dim light of strange stars. The wind fluttered his black cloak and the hood that half shadowed and now half revealed his almost fleshless face.

"There, do you see it, lads?"

"What?"

"The Undiscovered Country. Out there. Look long, look deep, make a feast. The Past, boys, the Past. Oh, it's dark, yes, and full of nightmare. Everything that Halloween ever was lies buried there. Will you dig for bones, boys? Do you have the *stuff?*"

He burned his gaze at them.

"What *is* Halloween? How did it start? Where? Why? What for? Witches, cats, mummy dusts, haunts. It's all there in that country from which no one returns. Will you dive into the dark ocean, boys? Will you fly in the dark sky?"

The boys swallowed hard.

Someone peeped: "We'd like to, but—Pipkin. We've got to wait for Pipkin."

"Yeah, Pipkin sent us to your place. We couldn't go without *him.*"

As if summoned in this instant they heard a cry from the far side of the ravine.

"Hey! Here I *am!*" called a frail voice. They saw his small figure standing with a lit pumpkin, on the far ravine ledge.

"This way!" they all yelled. "Pipkin! Quick!"

"Coming!" was the cry. "I don't feel so good. But—I had to come—wait for me!"

Chapter 6

They saw his small figure run down the middle of the ravine, on the path.

"Oh, wait, please wait—" the voice began to fail. "I don't feel well. I can't run. Can't—can't—"

"Pipkin!" everyone shouted, waving from the edge of the cliff.

His figure was small, small, small. There were shadows mixed everywhere. Bats flew. Owls shrieked. Night ravens clustered like black leaves in trees.

The small boy, running with his lit pumpkin, fell.

"Oh," gasped Moundshroud.

The pumpkin light went out.

"Oh," gasped everyone.

"Light your pumpkin, Pip, light it!" shrieked Tom.

He thought he saw the small figure scrabbling in the dark grass below, trying to strike a light. But in that instant of darkness, the night swept in. A great wing folded over the abyss. Many owls hooted. Many mice scampered and slithered in the shadows. A million tiny murders happened somewhere.

"Light your pumpkin, Pip!"

"Help—" wailed his sad voice.

A thousand wings flew away. A great beast beat the air somewhere like a thumping drum.

The clouds, like gauzy scenes, were pulled away to set a clean sky. The moon was there, a great eye.

It looked down upon—

An empty path.

Pipkin nowhere to be seen.

Way off, toward the horizon, something dark frittered and danced and slithered away in the cold star air.

"Help—help—" wailed a fading voice.

Then it was gone.

"Oh," mourned Mr. Moundshroud. "This

is bad. I fear Something has taken him away."

"Where, where?" gibbered the boys, cold.

"To the Undiscovered Country. The Place I wanted to show you. But now—"

"You don't mean that Thing in the ravine, It, or Him, or whatever, that Something, was— Death? Did he grab Pipkin and—*run?!*"

"Borrowed is more like it, perhaps to hold him for ransom," said Moundshroud.

"Can Death do that?"

"Sometimes, yes."

"Oh, gosh." Tom felt his eyes water. "Pip, tonight, running slow, so pale. Pip, you should-n't've come out!" he shouted at the sky, but there was only wind there and white clouds floating like old spirit fluff, and a clear river of wind.

They stood, cold, shivering. They looked off to where the Dark Something had stolen their friend.

"So," said Moundshroud. "All the more rea-son for you to come along, lads. If we fly fast, maybe we can catch Pipkin. Grab his sweet Halloween corn-candy soul. Bring him back, pop him in bed, toast him warm, save his breath. What say, lads? Would you solve two-mysteries-

43

in-one? Search and seek for lost Pipkin, and solve Halloween, all in one fell dark blow?"

They thought of All Hallows' Night and the billion ghosts awandering the lonely lanes in cold winds and strange smokes.

They thought of Pipkin, no more than a thimbleful of boy and sheer summer delight, torn out like a tooth and carried off on a black tide of web and horn and black soot.

And, almost as one, they murmured: "Yes."

Moundshroud sprang. He ran. He pummeled, he pushed, he raved. "Quick now, along this path, up this rise, along this road! The abandoned farm! Over the fence! Allez-oop!"

They leaped the fence running and stood by a barn that was frosted over with old circus posters, with banners tattered by wind pasted here thirty, forty, fifty years back. Circuses, passing through, had left patches and swatches of themselves ten inches thick.

"A kite, boys. Build a kite. Quick!"

Chapter 7

No sooner had he cried this than Mr. Mound-shroud ripped a great tissue from the side of the barn! It fluttered in his hands: the eye of a tiger! Another rip from another ancient poster and—the mouth of a lion!

The boys heard roars of Africa down the wind.

They blinked. They ran. They scratched with fingernails. They plucked with hands. They seized off strips and patches and huge rolls of animal flesh, of fang, and piercing eye, of wounded flank, of blood-red claw, of tail, of bound and leap and cry. The whole side of the barn was an ancient parade stopped dead. They tore it asunder. And with each tear they pulled

45

off talon, tongue, or ravening feline eye. Beneath waited layer upon layer of jungle nightmare, delicious encounters with polar bears, panicked zebra, milling prides of lions, charging rhinos, clambering gorillas which pawed up the side of midnight and swung toward dawn. A thousand animals in congregation rumbled to be set free. Now free in fists and hands and fingers, whistling on the autumn wind, the boys raced off across the grass.

Now Moundshroud knocked down old fence-railing beams and made a rough kite-cross and bound them with wire, then stood back to receive the gifts of kite paper as the boys flung them in fistfuls.

And these he tossed in place upon the frame, and, spark-flinting, fused with burnings of his horny hands.

"Hey!" The boys cried their delight. "Oh, look!"

They had never seen such things, or known that men such as Moundshroud with a pinch, a clutch, a pressure of fingers might blend an eye with tooth, a tooth with mouth, a mouth with feline bobcat tail. All, all mingled beautifully into a single thing, a wild jigsaw puzzle jungle zoo billowed and trapped, pasted and tied, growing, growing, taking color and sound and pattern in the light of the ascending moon. Now another cannibal eye. Now another hungry maw. A mad chimpanzee. A most insane mandrill-ape. A screaming butcher bird! The boys ran up with the last frights handed over and the kite finished, the ancient flesh laid out, fused by the still blue-smoke-burning horny hands. Mr. Moundshroud lit a cigar with the last bit of fire that sparked out of his thumb and smiled. And the light from his smile showed the Kite for what it was, a kite of destructions, of animals so dire and fierce their outcry drowned the wind and murdered the heart.

He was pleased, the boys were pleased.

For the Kite somehow seemed to resemble . . .

"Why," said Tom, astounded, "a pterodactyl!"

"A *what?*"

"Pterodactyl, those ancient flying reptiles, gone some billion years back, and never seen again," replied Mr. Moundshroud. "Well said, boy. Pterodactyl it seems and is, and 'twill fly us downwind to Perdition or Lands End or some other fine-sounding place. But, now,

47

rope, twine, string, quick! Filch and carry!"

They ran the rope off an old abandoned clothes line strung between barn and abandoned farmhouse. A good ninety feet or more of rope they brought Moundshroud who snaked it through his fist until it smoked a most unholy smoke. He tied it to the middle of the vast Kite which flapped like a somehow lost and out-of-water manta ray upon this high strange beach. It struggled with wind to live. It flapped and floundered on the heaves of tidal air, laid down on grass.

Moundshroud stood back, gave a jerk, and lo! the Kite—flew!

It hung low upon the air at the end of its clothes line, in a dumb-brute groveling of wind, veering this way, dashing that, leaping up suddenly to confront them with a wall of eyes, a solid flesh of teeth, a storm of cries.

"It won't rise, won't go straight! A tail, we need a tail!"

And as by instinct Tom dived first, and seized the Kite by its bottom. He hung there. The Kite steadied. It began to rise.

"Yes," cried the dark man. "Oh lad, you are the one. Bright boy! You be the tail! And more, and more!"

And as the Kite slowly ascended the cold river of swift flowing air, each boy in turn, seized with the whim, spurred by his wits, became more and yet more of the tail. Which is to say that Henry-Hank, disguised as a Witch, grabbed Tom's ankles, and now the Kite had two boys for its magnificent tail!

And Ralph Bengstrum, wound up in his Mummy clothes, stumbling over his winding tapes, smothered in his burial rags, shambled forward, jumped, and grabbed Henry-Hank's ankles.

So three boys hung now in a Tail!

"Wait! Here I come!" cried Beggar, who under his dirt and rags was really Fred Fryer.

He jumped, he caught.

The Kite ascended. The four boys making the tail yelled for more length!

They got it when the boy dressed as an Ape-man scrambled and grabbed ankles followed by the boy dressed as Death with a Scythe who did dangerously likewise.

"Watch out with that scythe!"

The scythe fell and lay in the grass like a lost smile.

But the two boys hung down now from all

the half-washed ankles, and the Kite rose more, higher, higher adding a boy and a boy, and a boy until with a yell and shout, eight boys were downhung in a magnificent thrashing tail, the down-hung in a magnificent thrashing tail, the last two being Ghost who was truly George Smith and Wally Babb who had, inspired, made himself up to look like a Gargoyle fallen off the top of a cathedral.

The boys yelled with elation. The Kite swooped and—took off!

"Hey!"

Whoosh! The Kite purred with a thousand animal whispers.

Whannng! The Kite rope strummed the wind.

Hush! said the entire thing.

And the wind flew them high across the stars.

Leaving Moundshroud to look up with awe at his contraption, his kite, his boys.

"Wait!" he shouted.

"Don't wait, come on!" the boys yelled.

Moundshroud ran along the grass to seize the scythe. His cape fluttered taking air, making wings until he, also, very simply, took off, and soared.

Chapter 8

The Kite flew.

The boys hung down from the Kite in a fine lizard's tail, now weaving, now looping, now snapping, now gliding.

They yelled with delight. They shrieked with ingasped, outgasped terror. They rode across the moon in an exclamation point. They soared over hills and meadows and farms. They saw themselves reflected in dusky moon-bright streams, creeks, rivers. They brushed down over ancient trees. The wind stirred by their passing shook down whole government mints of coins, leaves, bright showering to the black-grassed earth. They flew over the town and thought—

O look up! see! here we are! your sons!

And thought: O look down, there somewhere are our mothers, fathers, brothers, sisters, teachers! Hey, here we are! O, someone, see us! or you'll never *believe!*

And in a last swoop the Kite whistled, hummed, drummed along the winds to float over the old house and the Halloween Tree where first they had met Moundshroud!

Swoomp, flutter, glide, rush, hiss!

The suction of their swung bodies caused a thousand candles to flutter, flicker, stutter their light, hiss with desire to reflame themselves, so all the hung pumpkin scowls and leers and wild smiles were half-snuffed to unhappy shadows. The whole Tree went dead for a heartbeat. Then as the Kite sang high—the Tree blazed up with a thousand new cut-pumpkin frowns, glares, grimaces, and grins!

The windows of the house, black mirrors, saw the Kite go away and away, until the boys and the Kite and Mr. Moundshroud were very small on the horizon.

And then down they sailed off away deep into the Undiscovered Country of Old Death and Strange Years in the Frightful Past. . . .

"Where are we going?" cried Tom, hanging to the Kite's tail.

"Yes, where, where?" cried all the boys, one after another, below, below.

"Not where, but when!" said Moundshroud, pacing them, his great veiled cloak full of moon-wind and time. "Two thousand, count them, years before Christ! Pipkin's there, waiting! I smell it! Fly!"

Then the moon began to blink. It closed up its eye and there was darkness. Then faster and faster it began to wink, to wax, to wane, to wax again. Until a thousand times over it flickered and in flickering changed the landscape below, and then fifty thousand times, so fast they could not see it, the moon extinguished and relit itself.

And the moon stopped winking and held very still.

And the land was changed.

"Look," said Moundshroud, hung upon the very air above them.

And the million tiger-lion-leopard-panther eyes of the autumn Kite looked down, as did the eyes of the boys.

And the sun rose showing them . . .

Egypt. The River Nile. The Sphinx. The Pyramids.

"But," said Moundshroud. "Notice anything —different?"

"Why," gasped Tom, "it's all *new*. It's just been built. That means we really *have* gone back in Time four thousand years!"

And, sure enough, the Egypt that lay below was ancient sand but new-cut stone. The Sphinx, with its great lion paws treaded out on the golden stuffs of desert, was sharp-cut and freshly born out of the womb of stone mountains. It was a vast pup in the bright and empty glare of noon. If the sun had fallen and lay between its paws, it would have cuffed it like a fireball toy.

The Pyramids? Why they lay like strange-shaped blocks, yet other games to be puzzled over, played with by the woman-lion Sphinx.

The Kite zoomed down and skirted the sand dunes, flirted over one pyramid and was drawn, as by suction, by an open tomb-mouth set in a small cliff.

"Hey, Presto!" cried Moundshroud.

With a flap he gave the Kite such a kick as

made the boys toll like clamorous bells.

"Hey, no!" they cried.

The Kite shuddered, fell down, hovered ten feet above the dunes, and shook itself like a wild dog ridding itself of fleas.

The boys fell safe in golden sand.

The Kite broke away in a thousand shreds of eyes, fangs, shrieks, roars, elephant trumpetings. The Egyptian tomb-mouth sucked them in, and Moundshroud, laughing, with it.

"Mr. Moundshroud, wait!"

Leaping up, the boys ran to shout into the dark tomb doorway. Then they lifted their gaze and saw where they were.

The Valley of the Kings, where huge stone gods loomed above. Dust sifted in a strange downpour of tears from their eyes; tears made of sand and powdered rock.

The boys leaned into the shadows. Like a dry river bottom, the corridors led down to deep vaults where lay the linen-wrapped dead. Dust fountains echoed and played in strange courtyards a mile below. The boys ached, listening. The tomb breathed out a sick exhalation of paprika, cinnamon, and powdered camel dung. Somewhere, a mummy dreamed, coughed in its sleep, unraveled a bandage, twitched its dusty tongue and turned over for another thousand-year snooze. . . .

"Mr. Moundshroud?" called Tom Skelton.

Chapter 9

And from deep in the dry earth a lost voice whispered:

"Mound—sssss—shroud."

Out of the darkness something rolled, rushed, flapped.

A long strip of mummy cloth snapped out into the sunlight.

It was as if the very tomb itself had stuck out its old dry tongue which lay at their feet.

The boys stared. The linen strip was hundreds of yards long and might, if they wished, lead them down, down into the mysterious deeps below the Egyptian earth.

Tom Skelton, trembling, put one toe out to touch the yellow linen strip.

A wind blew from the tombs, saying: Yessss—"

"Here I go," said Tom.

And, balancing on the tightrope of linen, he wandered down and vanished in the dark under the burial chambers.

"Yesssss—!" whispered the wind coming up from below. "All of you. Come. Next. And next. And another and another. Quick."

The boys raced down the linen path in darkness.

"Watch for murder, boys! Murder!"

The pillars on both sides of the rushing boys flashed to life. Pictures shivered and moved.

The golden sun was on every pillar.

But it was a sun with arms and legs, bound tight with mummy wrappings.

"Murder!"

A dark creature struck the sun one dreadful blow.

The sun died. Its fires went out.

The boys ran blind in darkness.

Yeah, thought Tom, running, sure, I mean, I think, every night, the sun dies. Going to sleep, I wonder, will it come back? Tomorrow morning, will it still be dead?

The boys ran. On new pillars dead-ahead, the

sun appeared again, burning out of eclipse.
Swell! thought Tom. That's it! Sunrise!

But just as quickly, the sun was murdered
again. On each pillar they raced by, the sun
died in autumn and was buried in cold winter.

Middle of December, thought Tom, I often
think: the sun'll never come back! Winter will
go on forever! This time the sun is *really* dead!

But as the boys slowed at the end of the long
corridor, the sun was reborn. Spring arrived
with golden horns. Light filled the corridor
with pure fire.

The strange God stood burning on every wall,
his face a grand fire of triumph, wrapped in
golden ribbons.

"Why, heck, I know who *that* is!" panted
Henry-Hank. "Saw him in a movie once with
terrible Egyptian mummies!"

"Osiris!" said Tom.

"Yesssssssss . . ." hissed Moundshroud's voice
from the deep tombs. "Lesson Number One
about Halloween. Osiris, Son of the Earth and
Sky, killed each night by his brother Darkness.
Osiris slain by Autumn, murdered by his own
night blood.

"So it goes in every country. Each has its

death festival, having to do with seasons. Skulls and bones, boys, skeletons and ghosts. In Egypt, lads, see the Death of Osiris, King of the Dead. Gaze long."

The boys gazed.

For they had come to a vast hole in the underground cavern and through this hole they could look out at an Egyptian village where, at dusk, food was being placed out in pottery and copper dishes on porches and sills.

"For the homecoming ghostsssssss," whispered Moundshroud somewhere in the shadows.

Rows of oil lamps were nailed to house fronts and the soft smoke from these rose up on the twilight air like wandering spirits.

You could almost see the haunts shifting along the cobbled streets.

The shadows leaned away from the lost sun in the west and tried to enter the houses.

But the warm food, steaming on the porches, kept the shadows circling and stirring.

A faint smell of incense and mummy dust wafted up to the boys who looked out upon this ancient Halloween and the "treats" being set forth not for wandering boys but homeless ghosts.

"Hey," whispered all the boys.

"Do not lose your way in the dark," voices sang in the houses, to harps and lutes. "O dear sweet dead, come home, and welcome here. Lost in the dark but always dear. Do not wander, do not roam. Dear ones, come home."

Smoke curled from the dim lamps.

And the shadows stepped up on the porches and, very gently, touched the gifts of food.

And in one house they could see an old grandfather mummy being taken out of a closet and put in the place of honor at the head of the table, with food set before him. And the members of the family sat down to their evening meal and lifted their glasses and drank to the dead one seated there, all dust and dry silence....

Chapter 10

"Quick, now, come find me!"

Moundshroud's voice, laughing, called them on.

"This way! No, this! This!"

They ran along the slender ribbon of mummy wrapping, deep into the earth.

"Yes. Here I am."

They turned a corner and stopped, for the long linen ribbon wound across the tomb floor and up a wall to wrap around the feet of an ancient brown mummy which was propped atilt in a candlelit niche.

"Is," stuttered Ralph Bengstrum, dressed in his own Mummy costume, "is—is that a *real* mummy?"

"Yes." Dust sifted from under the golden mask on the mummy's face. "Real."

"Mr. Moundshroud! *You!*"

The gold mask fell to clang like a bright bell on the floor.

Where the mask had been was a mummy's face, a pool of brown mud crinkled by blasts of sun. One eye was glued shut with spiderweb. The other eye cracked forth tears of dust and a glint of bright blue glass.

"Isssss there some boy there dressed like a mummy?" asked the voice muffled beneath the shroud.

"Why, me, sir!" squeaked Ralph, showing his arms, legs, chest, the medical bandages it had taken him all afternoon to wrap himself up in, mummified.

"Good," sighed Moundshroud. "Grab the linen strip. Pull!"

Ralph bent, took hold of the ancient mummy bandages and—yanked!

The ribbon unraveled up around, up around to reveal the great ancient reptile nose-beak and flaky chin and dry smiling dust-powdery mouth of Moundshroud. His crossed arms fell loose.

"Thanks, lad! Free! No fun being wrapped

like some old funeral gift for the Land of the Dead. But—hist! Quick, boys, hop in the niches, stand stiff. Someone's coming. Play mummies, boys, play *dead!*"

The boys leaped to stand, arms folded, eyes shut, breaths held, like a frieze of small mummies cut in the ancient rock.

"Easy," whispered Moundshroud. "Here comes—"

A funeral procession.

An army of mourners in gold and fine silks bearing small sailing-ship toys and copper bowls of food in their hands.

And in their midst, a mummy case carried light as sunshine on the shoulders of six men. And behind that, a fresh-wrapped mummy with new paintings on its linen vestments and a small gold mask fitted over the hidden face.

"See the food, boys, the toys," whispered Moundshroud. "They put toys in the tombs, lads. So the gods will come play, romp, roustabout, and run children happy to the Land of the Dead. See the boats, kites, jump-ropes, toy knives—"

"But look at the size of that mummy," said Ralph, inside his hot linen bandages. "It's a twelve-year-old boy in there! Like me! And that gold mask on the boy mummy's face—doesn't it look familiar?"

"Pipkin!" cried everyone, hoarsely.

"Sh!" hissed Moundshroud.

For the funeral had stopped, the high priests were glancing around through the flickering torch shadows.

The boys, high in their niches, squeezed their eyes tight, sucked in their breaths.

"Not a whisper," said Moundshroud, a mosquito in Tom's ear. "Not a murmur."

The harp music began again.

The funeral shuffled on.

And in the midst of all the gold and toys, the kites of the dead, there was the small twelve-year-old fresh-new mummy with a gold mask that looked just exactly like—

Pipkin.

No, no, no, no! thought Tom.

"Yes!" cried a mouse voice, tiny, lost, wrapped away, kept, trapped, wild. *"It's me! I'm here. Under the mask. Under the wrappings. Can't move! Can't yell. Can't fight free!"*

Pipkin! thought Tom. Wait!

"Can't help it! Trapped!" shouted the small

wee voice wrapped in picture linens. *"Follow! Meet me! Find me at—"*

The voice faded, for the funeral procession had turned a corner in the dark labyrinth and was gone.

"Follow you where, Pipkin?" Tom Skelton jumped down from his niche and yelled into the dark. "Meet you *where?*"

But at that exact moment, Moundshroud, like a chopped tree, fell out of his niche. Bang! he struck the floor.

"Wait!" he cautioned Tom, looking up at him with one eye that looked like a spider caught in its own web. "We'll save old Pipkin yet. Sly does it. Slide and creep, boys. Ssst."

They helped him up and unwound some of his mummy wrappings and tiptoed down the long corridor and turned the corner.

"Holy Cow," whispered Tom. "Look. They're putting Pipkin's mummy in the coffin and the coffin inside the—the—"

"Sarcophagus," Moundshroud supplied the jawcracker. "A coffin in a coffin in a coffin, lad. Each larger than the last, all done up in hieroglyphs to tell his life story—"

"*Pipkin's* life?" said all.

69

"Or whoever Pipkin was this time around, this year, four thousand years ago."

"Yeah," whispered Ralph. "Look at the pictures on the sides of the coffin. Pipkin one year old. Pipkin five. Pipkin ten and running fast. Pipkin up an apple tree. Pipkin pretending to drown in the lake. Pipkin eating his way through a peach orchard. Wait, what's *that?*"

Moundshroud watched the busy funeral. "They're putting furniture in the tomb for him to use in the Land of the Dead. Boats. Kites. Tops to spin. Fresh fruits should Pipkin wake a hundred years from now, hungry."

"He'll be hungry all right. Good grief, look, they're going out! They're closing the tomb!" Moundshroud had to grab and hold Tom for he was jumping up and down in agony. "Pipkin's still in there, buried! When do we save him?"

"Later. The Long Night is young. We'll see Pipkin again, never fear. Then—"

The tomb door slammed shut.

The boys yammered and yelled. In the dark they could hear the scrape and slosh of mortar filling the last cracks and seams as the final stones were shoved in place.

The mourners went away with their silent harps.

Ralph stood in his Mummy costume, stunned, watching the last shadows go.

"Is that why I'm dressed like a mummy?" He fingered the bandages. He touched his clay-wrinkled ancient face. "Is that what my part of Halloween is all *about*?"

"All, boy, all," murmured Moundshroud. "The Egyptians, why, they built to last. Ten thousand years they planned for. Tombs, boys, tombs. Graves. Mummies. Bones. Death, death. Death was at the very heart, gizzard, light, soul, and body of their life! Tombs and more tombs with secret passages, so none might be found, so grave robbers could not borrow souls and toys and gold. You are a mummy, boy, because that was how they dressed for Eternity. Spun up in a cocoon of threads, they hoped to come forth like lovely butterflies in some far dear loving world. Know your cocoon, boy. Touch the strange stuffs."

"Why," said Ralph the Mummy, blinking at the smoky walls and old hieroglyphics. "*Every* day was Halloween to them!"

"Every day!" gasped all, in admiration.

71

"Every day was Halloween for *them,* too." Moundshroud pointed.

The boys turned.

A kind of green electric storm simmered in the tomb dungeon. The ground shuddered as with an ancient earthquake. Somewhere, a volcano turned over in its sleep, lighting the walls with one fiery shoulder.

And on the walls beyond were prehistoric drawings of cavemen, long before the Egyptians.

"Now," said Moundshroud.

Lightning struck.

Saber-toothed tigers caught the cavemen screaming. Tarpits drowned their bones. They sank, wailing.

"Wait. Let's save a few with fire."

Moundshroud blinked. Lightning struck to burn forests. One apeman, running, seized a burning branch and rammed it in a saber-tooth's jaws. The tiger shrieked and fell away. The apeman, snorting in triumph, tossed the fiery branch into a pile of autumn leaves in his cave. Other men came to hold their hands out to the fire, laughing at the night where the yellow beast eyes waited, afraid.

"See, boys?" Moundshroud's face flickered

with the fire. "The days of the Long Cold are done. Because of this one brave, new-thinking man, summer lives in the winter cave."

"But?" said Tom. "What's that got to do with Halloween?"

"Do? Why, blast my bones, everything. When you and your friends die every day, there's no *time* to think of Death, is there? Only time to run. But when you stop running at long last—"

He touched the walls. The apemen froze in mid-flight.

"—now you have time to think of where you came from, where you're going. And fire lights the way, boys. Fire and lightning. Morning stars to gaze at. Fire in your own cave to protect you. Only by night fires was the caveman, beast-man, able at last to turn his thoughts on a spit and baste them with wonder. The sun died in the sky. Winter came on like a great white beast shaking its fur, burying him. Would spring ever come back to the world? Would the sun be re-born next year or stay murdered? Egyptians asked it. Cavemen asked it a million years before. *Will* the sun rise tomorrow morning?"

"And *that's* how Halloween began?"

"With such long thoughts at night, boys. And

always at the center of it, fire. The sun. The sun dying down the cold sky forever. How that must have scared early man, eh? That was the Big Death. If the sun went away forever, *then* what?

"So in the middle of autumn, everything dying, apemen turned in their sleep, remembered their own dead of the last year. Ghosts called in their heads. Memories, that's what ghosts are, but apemen didn't know that. Behind their eyelids, late nights, the memory ghosts called, waved, danced, so apemen woke up, tossed twigs on the fire, shivered, wept. They could drive away wolves but not memories, not ghosts. So they held tight to their ribs, prayed for spring, watched the fire, thanked invisible gods for harvests of fruit and nuts.

"Halloween, indeed! A million years ago, in a cave in autumn, with ghosts inside heads, and the sun lost."

Moundshroud's voice faded.

He unraveled another yard or two of mummy wrappings, draped them over his arm grandly and said: "More to see. Come on, boys."

And they walked out of the catacombs into the twilight of an old Egyptian day.

A great pyramid lay before them, waiting.

"Last one to the top," said Moundshroud, "is a monkey's uncle!"

And the monkey's uncle was Tom.

Chapter 11

Gasping, they reached the pyramid's top where waited a vast crystal lens, a viewing glass which spun slowly in the wind on a golden tripod, a gigantic eye with which to bring far places near.

In the west, the sun, smothered and dying in clouds, sank. Moundshroud hooted his delight:

"There it goes, boys. The heart, soul, and flesh of Halloween. The Sun! There Osiris is murdered again. There sinks Mithras, the Persian fire. There falls Phoebus Apollo all Grecian light. Sun and flame, boys. Look and blink. Turn that crystal spyglass. Swing it down the Mediterranean Coast a thousand miles. See the Greek Isles?"

"Sure," said plain George Smith, dressed up

as fancy pale ghost. "Cities, towns, streets,
houses. People jumping out on porches to bring
food!"

"Yes." Moundshroud beamed. "*Their* Festival of the Dead: *the Feast of Pots*. Trick-or-
Treat old style. But tricks from the dead if you
don't feed them. So treats are laid out in fine
banquets on the sill!"

Far away, in the sweet dusk, smells of cooked
meats steamed, dishes were dealt out for spirits
that smoked across the land of the living. The
women and children of the Grecian homes
came and went with multitudinous quantities
of spiced and delectable victuals.

Then, all through the Grecian Isles, doors
slammed. The vast slamming echoed along the
dark wind.

"The temples shutting tight," said Moundshroud. "Every holy place in Greece will be
double-locked this night."

"And look!" Ralph-who-was-a-Mummy swung
the crystal lens. The light flared over the boys'
masks. "Those people, why are they painting
black molasses on their front door posts?"

"Pitch," corrected Moundshroud. "Black tar

to glue the ghosts, stick them fast, so they *can't* get inside."

"Why," said Tom, "didn't *we* think of that!?"

Darkness moved down the Mediterranean shores. From the tombs, like mist, the dead spirits wavered in soot and black plumes along the streets to be caught in the dark tar that smeared the porch sills. The wind mourned, as if telling the anguish of the trapped dead.

"Now, Italy. Rome." Moundshroud turned the lens to see Roman cemeteries where people placed food on graves and hurried off.

The wind whipped Moundshroud's cape. It hollowed his mouth:

> *"O autumn winds that bake and burn*
> *And all the world to darkness turn,*
> *Now storm and seize and make of me . . .*
> *A swarm of leaves from Autumn's Tree!"*

He kick-jumped straight up in the air. The boys yelled delight, even as his clothes, cape, hair, skin, body, corn-candy bones tore apart before their eyes.

"... *leaves* ... *burn* ...
... *change* ... *turn* ...!"

The wind ribboned him to confetti; a million autumn leaves, gold, brown, red as blood, rust, all wild, rustling, simmering, a clutch of oak and maple leaf, a hickory leaf downfall, a toss of flaking whisper, murmur, rustle to the dark river-creek sky. Not one kite, but ten thousand thousand tiny mummy-flake kites, Moundshroud exploded apart:

"*World turn! Leaves burn!
Grass die! Trees ... fly!*"

And from a billion other trees in autumn lands, leaves rushed to join with the upflung battalions of dry bits that were Moundshroud dispersed in whirlwinds from which his voice stormed:

"Boys, see the fires along the Mediterranean coast? Fires burning north through Europe? Fires of fear. Flames of celebration. Would you spy, boys? Up, now, fly!"

And the leaves in avalanche fell upon each boy like terrible flapping moths and carried them away. Over Egyptian sands they sang and laughed and giggled. Over the strange sea, rapturous and hysterical, they soared.

"Happy New Year!" a voice cried, far below.

"Happy *what?*" asked Tom.

"Happy New Year!" Moundshroud, a flock of rusty leaves, rustled his voice. "In old times, the first of November was New Year's Day. The true end of summer, the cold start of winter. Not exactly happy, but, well, Happy New Year!"

They crossed Europe and saw new water below.

"The British Isles," whispered Moundshroud. "Would you cock an eye at England's own druid God of the Dead?"

"We would!"

"Quiet as milkweed, then, soft as snow, fall, blow away down, each and all."

The boys fell.

Like a bushel of chestnuts, their feet rained to earth.

Chapter 12

Now the boys who landed like a downpour of bright autumn trash were in this order:

Tom Skelton, dressed up in his delicious Bones.

Henry-Hank, more or less a Witch.

Ralph Bengstrum, an unraveled Mummy, becoming more unbandaged by the minute.

A Ghost named George Smith.

J.J. (no other name needed) a very fine Apeman.

Wally Babb who said he was a Gargoyle, but everyone said he looked more like Quasimodo.

Fred Fryer, what else but a beggar fresh out of a ditch.

And last and not least, "Hackles" Nibley who had run up a costume at the last moment by simply clapping on a white scare-mask and grabbing his grandpa's harvest scythe off the garage wall.

All the boys being safely landed on English earth, their billion autumn leaves fell off and blew away.

They stood in the midst of a vast field of wheat.

"Here, Master Nibley, I brought your scythe. Take it. Grab! Now lie low!" warned Moundshroud. "The Druid God of the Dead! Samhain! Fall!"

They fell.

For a huge scythe came skimming down out of the sky. With its great razor edge it cut the wind. With its whistling side it sliced clouds. It beheaded trees. It razored along the cheek of the hill. It made a clean shave of wheat. In the air a whole blizzard of wheat fell.

And with every whisk, every cut, every scythe, the sky was aswarm with cries and shrieks and screams.

The scythe hissed up.

The boys cowered.

"Hunh!" grunted a large voice.

"Mr. Moundshroud, is that *you!*" cried Tom.

For towering forty feet above them in the sky, an immense scythe in his hands, was this cowled figure, its face in midnight fogs.

The blade swung down: *hisssssss!*

"Mr. Moundshroud, let us be!"

"Shut up." Someone knocked Tom's elbow. Mr. Moundshroud lay on the earth beside him. "That's not me. That's—"

"Samhain!" cried the voice in the fog. "God of the Dead! I harvest thus, and so!"

Sssss-whoooshhhh!

"All those who died this year are here! And for their sins, this night, are turned to *beasts!*"

Ssssssswooommmmmmm!

"Please," whimpered Ralph-the-Mummy.

"Sssssssstttt! The scythe zippered Hackles Nibley's spine, ripping his costume in a long tear, knocking his own small scythe free of his hands.

"Beasts!"

And the harvest wheat, flailed up, spun round on the wind, shrieking its souls, all those who had died in the past twelve months, rained

85

to earth. And falling, touching, the heads of wheat were turned to asses, chickens, snakes which scurried, cackled, brayed; were turned to dogs and cats and cows that barked, cried, bawled. But all were miniature. All were tiny, small, no bigger than worms, no bigger than toes, no bigger than the sliced-off tip of a nose. By the hundreds and thousands the wheat heads snowed up in scatters and fell down as spiders which could not shout or beg or weep for mercy, but which, soundless, raced over the grass, poured over the boys. A hundred centipedes tiptoed on Ralph's spine. Two hundred leeches clung to Hackles Nibley's scythe until with a nightmare gasp he raved and shook them off. Everywhere fell black widows and tiny boa constrictors.

"For your sins! Your sins! Take that! And this!" bellowed the voice in the whistling sky.

The scythe flashed. The wind, cut, fell in bright thunders. The wheat churned and gave up a million heads. Heads fell. Sinners hit like rocks. And, hitting, were turned to frogs and toads and multitudes of scaly warts with legs and jellyfish which stank in the light.

"I'll be good!" prayed Tom Skelton.

"Lemme live!" added Henry-Hank.

All of this said very loudly, for the scythe was making a dreadful roar. It was like an ocean wave falling down out of the sky, cleaning a beach, and running away up to cut more clouds. Even the clouds seemed to be whispering out swift and more fervent prayers for their own fates. Not me! not me!

"For all the evil you ever did!" said Samhain.

And the scythe cut and the souls were harvested and fell in blind newts and awful bed-bugs and dreadful cockroaches to scuttle, limp, creep, scrabble.

"My gosh, he's a bug maker."

"Flea squasher!"

"Snake grinder-outer!"

"Roach transformer!"

"Fly keeper!"

"No! Samhain! October God. God of the Dead!"

Samhain stomped a great foot which tread a thousand bugs in the grass, trompled ten thousand tiny soul-beasts in the dust.

"I think," said Tom, "it's time we—"

"Ran?" suggested Ralph, not offhand.

"Shall we take a vote?"

The scythe hissed. Samhain boomed.

"Vote, heck!" said Moundshroud.

All jumped up.

"You there!" thundered the voice above them. "Come back!"

"No, sir, thanks," said one and then another.

And put right foot after left.

"I figure," said Ralph, panting, leaping, tears on his cheeks. "I been pretty good most of my life. I don't deserve to die."

"Hah-hnnh!" shouted Samhain.

The scythe came in a guillotine which chunked the head off an oak tree and felled a maple. A whole orchard of autumn apples fell into a marble pit somewhere. It sounded like a houseful of boys falling downstairs.

"I don't think he heard you, Ralph," said Tom.

They dived. They fell among rocks and shrubs.

The scythe richocheted off the stones.

Samhain gave such a yell as brought an avalanche down a small hill nearby.

"Boy," said Ralph, squinched up, balled up, feet against chest, eyes tight. "England is no place to be a sinner."

Even as a final rain, a shower, a downpour of hysterical souls-turned-bettle, turned flea, turned stinkbug, turned daddy long-legs, scurried over the boys.

"Hey, look. That dog!"

A wild dog, mad with terror, raced up the rocks.

And its face, its eyes, something *in* the eyes—

"That couldn't be—?"

"Pipkin?" said everyone.

"Pip—" shouted Tom. "Is this where we *meet* you? Is—"

But *whoom!* The scythe fell.

And yipping with fright, the dog, bowled over, slid down the grass.

"Hold on, Pipkin. We know you, we see you! Don't scare off! Don't—" Tom whistled.

But the dog, yarping with Pipkin's own dear sweet scared voice, was gone.

But didn't an echo of his yip come back from the hills:

"Meet. Meet. Meet. Meeee . . ."

Where? thought Tom. Criminently, *where?*

Chapter 13

Samhain, scythe uplifted, gazed all about, happy at his games.

He chuckled a most delicious chuckle, spat fiery spittle on his horny hands, clenched the scythe tighter, swung it up, and froze. . . .

For somewhere, someone was singing.

Somewhere near the top of a hill, in a small clump of trees, a small bonfire flickered.

Men like shadows were gathered there, lifting up their arms and chanting.

Samhain listened, his scythe like a great smile in his arms.

"O Samhain, God of the Dead!
Hear us!

We the Holy Druid Priests in
This Grove of Trees, the great Oaks,
Plead for the Souls of the Dead!"

Far away, these strange men by their bright
fire lifted metal knives, lifted cats and goats in
their hands, chanting:

> *"We pray for the souls of those*
> *Who are turned to Beasts.*
> *O God of the Dead, we sacrifice*
> *These beasts*
> *So that you will let free*
> *The souls of our loved ones*
> *Who died this year!"*

The knives flashed.

Samhain smiled an even greater smile. The
animals shrieked.

All around the boys on the earth, the grass,
the rocks, the trapped souls, lost in spiders,
locked in roaches, put away in fleas and pillbugs and centipedes, gaped and yammered silent yammers and twitched and roiled.

Tom winced. He thought he heard a million
small, oh very microscopic, bleats of pain and

release from around him where the centipedes capered, spiders danced.

"Let free! Let be!" prayed the druids on the hill.

The fire blazed.

A sea wind roared over the meadows, brushed the rocks, touched at the spiders, rolled the pillbugs, tumbled the roaches. The tiny spiders, insects, the miniature dogs and cows fluffed away like a million snowflakes. The tiny souls trapped in insect bodies dissolved.

Released, with a vast cavern whisper, they whistled up the sky.

"To Heaven!" cried the druid priests. "O free! Go!"

They flew. They vanished in the air with a great sigh of thanks and much gratitude.

Samhain, God of the Dead, shrugged, and let them go. Then, just as suddenly, he stiffened.

As did the hidden boys and Mr. Mound-shroud, crouched in the rocks.

Through a valley and across the hill ran an army of Roman soldiers, a troop on the double. Their leader ran before them, shouting:

"Soldiers of Rome! Destroy the pagans! Destroy the unholy religion! Seutonius so orders!"

"For Seutonius!"

Samhain, in the sky, raised his scythe, too late!

The soldiers slammed swords and axes into the bases of the holy druid oaks.

Samhain shrieked in pain as if the axes had chopped his knees. The holy trees groaned, whistled, and, with a final chop, thundered to earth.

Samhain trembled in the high air.

The druid priests, fleeing, stopped and shuddered.

Trees fell.

The priests, chopped at the ankles, the knees, fell. They were blown over like oaks in a hurricane.

"No!" roared Samhain in the high air.

"But yes!" cried the Romans. "Now!"

The soldiers gave a final mighty blow.

And Samhain, God of the Dead, torn at his roots, chopped at his ankles, began to fall.

The boys, staring up, leaped out of the way. For it was like a giant forest falling all in one fall. They were shadowed by his midnight descent. The thunder of his death came before him. He was the greatest tree in all existence ever, the tallest oak ever to plummet down and die. Down he came through the wild air, screaming, flailing to hold himself up.

Samhain hit the earth.

He dropped with a roar that shook the bones of the hills and snuffed the holy fires.

And with Samhain cut and down and dead, the last of the druid oaks fell with him, like wheat cut with a final scythe. His own huge scythe, a vast smile lost in the fields, dissolved into a puddle of silver and sank into the grass.

Silence. A smoldering of fires. A blowing of leaves.

Instantly the sun went down.

The druid priests bled in the grass as the boys watched and the Roman captain prowled the dead fires kicking the holy ashes.

"Here we shall build our temples to our gods!"

The soldiers lit new fires and burned incense before golden idols which they set in place.

But, no sooner lit, than a star shone in the east. On far desert sands, to camel bells, Three Wise Men moved.

The Roman soldiers lifted their bronze shields against the glare of the Star in the sky.

But their shields melted. The Roman idols melted and became shapes of Mary and her Son.

The soldiers' armor melted, dripped, changed. They were dressed now in the garments of priests who sang Latin before yet newer altars, even as Moundshroud, crouched, squinting, weighed the scene, and whispered it to his small masked friends:

"Aye, boys, see? Gods following gods. The Romans cut the Druids, their oaks, their God of the Dead, bang! down! And put in their own gods, eh? Now the Christians run and cut the Romans down! New altars, boys, new incense, new names . . ."

The wind blew the altar candles out.

In darkness, Tom cried out. The earth shuddered and spun. Rain drenched them.

"What's happening, Mr. Moundshroud? Where are we?"

Moundshroud struck a flinty thumb into fire and held it up. "Why, bless me, boys. It's the Dark Ages. The longest darkest night ever. Christ long since come and gone in the world and—"

"Where's Pipkin?"

"Here!" cried a voice from the black sky. "I think I'm on a broom! It's taking me—away!"

"Hey, me too," said Ralph and then J.J., and then Hackles Nibley, and Wally Babb, and all the rest.

There was a huge whisper like a gigantic cat stroking its whiskers in the dark.

"Brooms," muttered Moundshroud. "The gathering of the Brooms. The October Broom Festival. The annual Migration."

"To Where?" asked Tom, calling up, for everyone was making traffic on the air now in whisking shrieks.

"The Broom Works, of course!"

"Help! I'm flying!" said Henry-Hank.

Whisk. A broom whistled him away.

A great brambly cat flashed by Tom's cheek. He felt a wooden pole between his legs jump up.

"Hang on!" said Moundshroud. "When attacked by a broom, only one thing to do, hold tight!"

"I'm holding!" cried Tom, and flew away.

Chapter 14

The sky was swept clean with brooms.

The sky was yelled clean by boys occupying at least eight of those brooms at once.

And what with changing their cries of fear to cries of delight, the boys almost forgot to look or listen for Pipkin, similarly sailed off among island clouds.

"This way!" announced Pipkin.

"As quick as we can!" said Tom Skelton. "But, Pip, it's awful hard to ride a broomstick, I find!"

"Funny you say that," said Henry-Hank. "I agree."

Everyone agreed, falling off, hanging on, climbing back.

There was now such a hustle of brooms as
left no room for clouds, and none for mists and
certainly none for fog or boys. There was an
immense traffic jam of brooms, as if all earth's
forests gave up their branches in one boom
and fling and, scouring autumn fields, cut clean
and throttled tight such cereal grains as made
good sweepers, thrashers, beaters, then flew up.

So here came all the backyard washline prop-
poles in the world. And here came with them,
swatches of grass, clumps of weed, brambles

of bush to herd the sheep-clouds and cleanse the stars and ride the boys.

Said boys, each on his own skinny mount, were deluged with beatings and cuffings of flail and wood. They were punished severely for occupying heaven. They took a hundred bruises each, a dozen cuts, and precisely forty-nine lumps on their tender skulls.

"Hey, I got a bloody nose!" gasped Tom, happily, looking at the red on his fingers.

"Shucks!" cried Pipkin, going into a cloud dry and coming out wet. "That's nothing. I got one eye shut, one ear bad, and lost a tooth!"

"Pipkin!" called Tom. "Don't keep telling us to meet you and then we don't know where! *Where?*"

"In the air!" said Pipkin.

"Cheez," muttered Henry-Hank, "there's two zillion, one hundred billion, ninety-nine million acres of air wrapped around the world! Which half-acre does Pip mean?"

"I mean—" gasped Pipkin.

But a whole bundle of broomsticks banged up in an akimbo dance like a shuttle of cornstalks across his flight, or a farmland fence suddenly come antic and in frenzies.

A cloud with a grand fiend face gaped its mouth. It swallowed Pipkin, broom and all, then shut its vapors tight and rumbled with Pipkin indigestion.

"Kick your way out, Pipkin! Stomp him in the stomach!" someone suggested.

But nothing kicked and the cloud, satisfied, sailed on Forever's Bay toward Eternity's Dawn, ruminating over its delicious sweet boy-dinner.

"Meet him in the air?" Tom snorted. "Good grief, talk about horrible directions to nowhere."

"See even more horrible directions!" said Moundshroud, sailing by on a broom that looked like a wet and angry cat on the end of a mop. "Would you see witches, boys? Hags, crones, conjure wives, magicians, black magics, demons, devils? There they be, in mobs, in riots, boys. Skin your eyeballs."

And there below, all across Europe, through France and Germany and Spain, on the night roads were indeed clusters and mobs and parades of strange sinners running north, scrambling away from the Southern Sea.

"That's it! Jump, run! This way to the night. This way to the dark!" Moundshroud swooped low, shouting over the mobs like a general leading a fine, evil troop. "Quick, hide! Lie low. Wait a few centuries!"

"Hide out from what?" wondered Tom.

"Here come the Christians!" yelled voices below, on the roads.

And that was the answer.

Tom blinked and soared and watched.

And from all the roads the mobs ran to stand alone on farms, or at crossroads, in harvest fields, in towns. Old men. Old women. Toothless and raving, yelling to the sky as the brooms swept down.

"Why," said Henry-Hank, stunned. "Those are witches!"

"Dry-clean my soul and hang it out to dry if you're not right, boy," agreed Moundshroud.

"There are witches jumping fires," said J.J.

"And witches stirring cauldrons!" said Tom.

"And witches drawing symbols in farmyard dust!" said Ralph. Are they *real*? I mean, I always thought—"

"Real?" Moundshroud, insulted, almost fell from his bramble-cat broom. "Ye little gods and fishes, lad, every town has its resident witch. Every town hides some old Greek pagan priest, some Roman worshiper of tiny gods who ran up the roads, hid in culverts, sank in caves to escape the Christians! In every tiny village, boy, in every scrubby farm the old religions hide out. You saw the druids cut and chopped, eh? They hid from the Romans. And now the Romans, who fed Christians to lions, run themselves to hide. So all the little lollygaggin' cults, all flavors and types, scramble to survive. See how they run, boys!"

And it was true.

Fires burned all over Europe. At every crossroad and by every haystack dark forms jumped in cats across flames. Cauldrons bubbled. Old hags cursed. Dogs frolicked red-hot coals.

"Witches, witches, everywhere," said Tom, amazed. "I never knew they were so many!"

"Mobs and multitudes, Tom. Europe was flooded to the dikes. Witches underfoot, under bed, in the cellars and high attics."

"Boy oh boy," said Henry-Hank, proud in his Witch costume. "Real witches! Could they talk to the dead?"

"No," said Moundshroud.

"Jump up devils?"

"No."

"Keep demons in door hinges and squeal them out at midnight?"

"No."

"Ride broomsticks?"

"Nope."

"Put sneezing spells on people?"

"Sorry."

"Kill folks by sticking pins in dolls?"

"No."

"Well, heck, what *could* they do?"

"Nothing."

"Nothing!" cried all the boys, affronted.

"Oh, they *thought* they could, boys!"

Moundshroud led the Team down on their brooms over the farms where witches dropped frogs in cauldrons and stomped toads and snuffed mummy dust and cavorted in cackles.

"But, stop and think. What does the word 'witch' truly mean?"

"Why—" said Tom, and was stymied.

"Wits," said Moundshroud. "Intelligence. That's all it means. Knowledge. So any man, or woman, with half a brain and with inclinations toward learning had his wits about him, eh? And so, anyone too smart, who didn't watch out, was called—"

"A witch!" said everyone.

"And some of the smart ones, the ones with wits, pretended at magic, or dreamed themselves with ghosts and dead shufflers and ambling mummies. And if enemies dropped dead by coincidence, they took credit for it. They liked to believe they had power, but they had none, boys, none, sad and sorry, 'tis true. But listen. There beyond the hill. That's where the brooms come from. That's where they go."

The boys listened and heard:

> *"The Broomworks makes*
> *The Broom that looms*
> *On sky in gloom and rising of the moon*
> *That broom which, groom to witch, flies*
> *   high*
> *On harvestings of stormwind grass*
> *With shriek and sigh to motion it*
> *In ocean-seas of cloud, now soft, now*
> *   loud . . . !"*

Below, at full-tilt, a witch-broom factory was filled with commotions, poles being cut, and bound with broom-brushes which, no sooner

tied, took off up chimneys in flights of spark.
On rooftops, hags leaped on to ride the stars.

Or so it seemed, as the boys watched and
voices sang:

> *"Did witches feel the night wind in their*
>   *bed*
> *And reel and dance with devils and the*
>   *dead?*
> *No!*
> *But that is what they bragged and claimed*
>   *and said!*
> *Until whole continents, hellbent*
> *Named 'witches' of the Innocent,*
> *And did conspire*
> *To burn old women, babes, and virgins in*
>   *a fire."*

Mobs raved through villages and farms with
torches, cursing. Bonfires flared from the English Channel to the Mediterranean shore.

> *"Through all of Germany and France,*
> *Ten thousand so-called evil witches*
> *Hung to kick their final antic dance*

No village but what shared a dread uproar
As each side named the other for a devil's
> *pig,*
Old Satan's sow, the Demon's maddened
> *boar."*

Wild pigs, with witches glued to their backs, trotted roof tiles, flinting sparks, snorting steams:

> *"All Europe was a cloud of witches smoke.*
> *Their judges often bound and burnt with*
> > *them*
> *For what? A joke!*

> *"Until:* 'all men *are spoiled with guilt!*
> All *sin,* all *lie!'*
> *So, what to do?*
> *Why,* everyone *must die!"*

Smoke churned the sky. At every crossroads, witches hung, crows gathered in a feathered darkness.

The boys hung from their brooms in the sky, eyes popped, mouths wide.

"Anyone want to be a witch?" asked Mound-shroud, at last.

"Er," said Henry-Hank, shivering in his witch's rags, "n-not *me!*"

"No fun, eh, boy?"

"No fun."

The brooms flew them off through chars and smokes.

They landed on an empty street, in an open place, in Paris.

Their brooms fell over, dead.

Chapter 15

"Well, now, boys, what should we do to scare the scarers, frighten the frighteners, shiver the shiverers?" called Moundshroud inside a cloud. "What's bigger than demons and witches?"

"Bigger gods?"

"Bigger witches?"

"Bigger churches?" guessed Tom Skelton.

"Bless you, Tom, right! An idea gets big, yes? A religion gets big! How. With buildings large enough to cast shadows across an entire land. Build buildings you can see for a hundred miles. Build one so tall and famous it has a hunchback in it, ringing bells. So now, boys, help me build it brick by brick, flying buttress by flying buttress. Let's build—"

"Notre Dame!" shouted eight boys.

"And all the more reason to build Notre Dame because—" said Moundshroud." Listen—"

Bong!

A bell tolled in the sky.

Bong!

". . . help . . .!" whispered a voice when the sound had died.

Bong!

The boys looked and saw a kind of scaffolding reared up in half a belfry-keep upon the moon. At the very top hung a huge bronze bell that was tolling now.

And from inside that bell with every crash and bang and gong this small voice shouted:

"Help!"

The boys looked at Moundshroud.

Their eyes blazed a question:

Pipkin?

Meet me in the air! thought Tom. *And there he is!*

There, hung upside down over Paris, his head for a knocker, was Pipkin in a bell. Or the shadow, ghost, or lost spirit of Pipkin, anyway.

Which is to say there was a bell and when it

112

sounded the hour, why that sound was made by a flesh-and-blood clapper which knocked the rim. Pipkin's head banged the bell. Bong! And again: Bong!

"Knock his brains out," gasped Henry-Hank.

"Help!" called Pipkin, a shadow in the bell, a ghost chained upside down to strike the quarters and the hours.

"Fly!" cried the boys to their brooms, but their brooms lay dead on the Paris stones.

"No life in them," mourned Moundshroud. "Juice, sap, and fire all gone. Well, now." He rubbed his chin to sparks. "How do we get up to help Pipkin, with no brooms?"

"*You* fly, Mr. Moundshroud."

"Ah, no, that's not the ticket. You must save him, always and forever, again and again, this night, until one grand salvation. Wait. Ah! Inspiration. We were going to build Notre Dame, correct? Well then, let us by all means build it, there! and climb our way up to hard-skulled knock-the-bell sound-the-hour Pipkin! Hop it, lads! Climb those stairs!"

"*What* stairs?"

"These! Here! Here! And here!"

Bricks fell in place. The boys leaped. And as they put a foot up, out, and down, a stair came under it, one stone at a time.

Bong! said the bell.

Help! said Pipkin.

Feet galloping empty air came down to tap, rustle, clomp on—

A step. Another step.

And yet another and another climbing empty space.

Help! said Pipkin.

Bong! again went the hollow bell.

So they ran on emptiness, with Moundshroud prodding, shoving after. They ran on pure windy light only to have bricks and stones and mortar shuffle like cards, deal themselves solid, take form beneath their toes and heels.

It was like racing up through a cake that built itself layer on stone layer, and the wild bell and sad Pipkin shouting and pleading them on.

"Our shadow, there it is!" said Tom.

And indeed the shadow of this cathedral, this splendid Notre Dame, was tossed by moonlight all across France and half of Europe.

"Up, boys, up; no pause, no rest, run!"

Bong!

Help!

They ran. They began to fall with each step, but again and again and again steps came in place and saved them and ran them taller so the shadow of the spires loomed tall across rivers and fields to snuff the last witch fires at crossroads. Crones, hags, wise men, demon lovers, a thousand miles off, snuffed like candles, whiffed to smoke, wailed and sank to hide as the church leaned, tilted across the heavens.

"So even as the Romans cut down druid trees and chopped their God of the Dead to fall, we now with this church, boys, cast such a shadow as knocks all witches off their stilts, and puts seedy sorcerers and trite magicians to heel. No more small witch fires. Only this great lit candle, Notre Dame. Presto!"

The boys laughed with delight.

For the last step fell in place.

They had reached the top, gasping.

Notre Dame cathedral was finished and built.

Bong!

The last soft hour was struck.

The great bronze bell shuddered.

115

And hung empty.

The boys leaned to peer into its cavernous mouth.

There was no clapper inside shaped like Pipkin.

"Pipkin?" they whispered.

". . . kin," echoed the bell in a small echo.

"He's here somewhere. Up there in the air, meet him's what he promised. And Pipkin falls back on no promises," said Moundshroud. "Look about, boys. Fine handiwork, eh? Centuries of toil done in a fast gallop and sneeze, right? But, ah, ah, something beside Pipkin's missing. What? Glance up. Scan 'round. Eh?"

The boys peered. They puzzled.

"Er—"

"Don't the place look awful plain, boys? Awful untouched and unornamented?"

"Gargoyles!"

Everyone turned to look at . . .

Wally Babb, who was dressed as a Gargoyle for Halloween. His face fairly beamed with revelation.

"Gargoyles. The place's got no gargoyles."

"Gargoyles." Moundshroud uttered and ululated and beautifully ribboned the word with

116

his lizardly tongue. "Gargoyles. Shall we put them *on*, boys?"

"How?"

"Why I should think we could whistle them in place. Whistle for demons, boys, whistle for fiends, give a high tootling blow for beasties and ferocious fanged loomers of the dark."

Wally Babb sucked in a great breath. "Here's mine!"

He whistled.

All whistled.

And the gargoyles?

They came *running*.

Chapter 16

The unemployed of all midnight Europe shivered in their stone sleep and came awake.

Which is to say that all the old beasts, all the old tales, all the old nightmares, all the old unused demons-put-by, and witches left in the lurch, quaked at the call, reared at the whistle, trembled at the summons, and in dust devils of propulsion skimmed down the roads, flitted skies, buckshot through shaken trees, forded streams, swam rivers, pierced clouds, and arrived, arrived.

Which is still to say that all the dead statues and idols and semigods and demigods of Europe lying like a dreadful snow all about, abandoned, in ruins, gave a blink and start and came as

119

salamanders on the road, or bats in skies or din-
goes in the brush. They flew, they galloped,
they skittered.

To the general excitement and amazement
and much babbling shout from the fringe of
boys leaning out, Moundshroud leaning with
them as the mobs of strange beasts came from
north, south, east, west to panic at the gates and
wait for whistles.

"Shall we drop white-hot boiling lead down
on them?"

The boys saw Moundshroud's smile.

"Heck, no," said Tom. "Hunchback already
did that years ago!"

"Well, then, no burning lava. So shall we
whistle them up?"

They all whistled.

And obedient to summons, the mobs, the
flocks, the prides, the crush, the collection, the
raving flux of monsters, beasts, vices rampant,
virtues gone sour, discarded saints, misguided
prides, hollow pomps oozed, slid, suckered,
pelted, ran bold and right up the sides of Notre
Dame. In a floodtide of nightmare, in a tidal
wave of outcry and shamble they inundated the

cathedral, to crust themselves on every pinion and upthrust stone.

So here ran pigs and there climbed Satan's goats and yet another wall knew devils which recarved themselves along the way, dropped horns and grew new ones, shaved beards to sprout tendril earthworm mustaches.

Sometimes a swarm of only masks and faces scuttled up the walls and took the buttress heights, carried by an army of crayfish and wobbly-crotchety lobsters. Here came the heads of gorillas, full of sin and teeth. There came men's heads with sausages in their mouths. Beyond danced the mask of a Fool upheld by a spider that knew ballet.

So much was going on that Tom said: "My gosh, so much is going on!"

"And more to come, *there!*" said Moundshroud.

For now that Notre Dame was infested with various beasts and spidering leers and gloms and masks, why here came dragons chasing children and whales swallowing Jonahs and chariots chockful of skulls-and-bones. Acrobats and tumblers, yanked out of shape by demidemons, limped and fell in strange postures to freeze on the roof.

All accompanied by pigs with harps and sows with piccolos and dogs playing bagpipes, so the music itself helped charm and pull new mobs of grotesques up the walls to be trapped and caught forever in sockets of stone.

Here an ape plucked a lyre; there floundered a woman with a fish's tail. Now a sphinx flew out of the night, shed its wings and became woman and lion, half and half, settled to snooze away the centuries in the shadow and sound of high bells.

"Why, what are *those?*" cried Tom.

Moundshroud, leaning over, gave a snort: "Why those are Sins, boys! And nondescripts. There crawls the Worm of Conscience!"

They looked to see it crawl. It crawled very fine.

"Now," whispered Moundshroud softly. "Settle. Slumber. Sleep."

And the flocks of strange creatures turned about three times like evil dogs and lay down. All beasts took root. All grimaces froze to stone. All cries faded.

122

The moon shadowed and lit the gargoyles of Notre Dame.

"Does it make sense, Tom?"

"Sure. All the old gods, all the old dreams, all the old nightmares, all the old ideas with nothing to do, out of work, we *gave* them work. We *called* them here!"

"And here they will remain for centuries, right?"

"Right!"

They looked down over the rim.

There was a mob of beasts on the east battlement.

A crowd of sins on the west.

A surge of nightmares on the south.

And a fine scuttle of unnamed vices and ill-kept virtues to the north.

"I," said Tom, proud of this night's work, "wouldn't mind *living* here."

The wind crooned in the mouths of the beasts. Their fangs hissed and whistled: "Much thanks."

Chapter 17

"Jehosophat," said Tom Skelton, on the parapet. "We whistled all the stone griffins and demons here. Now Pipkin's lost again. I was thinking, why can't we whistle *him?*"

Moundshroud laughed so his cape boomed
on the night wind and his dry bones jangled inside his skin.

"Boys! Look around! He's still *here!*"

"Where?"

"Here," mourned a small faraway voice.

The boys crickled their spines looking over
the parapet, cracked their necks staring up.

"Look and find, lads, hide and seek!"

And even in seeking they could not help but
enjoy once more the turbulent slates of the ca-

thedral all fringed with horrors and deliciously ugly with trapped beasts.

Where was Pipkin among all those dark sea creatures with gills gaped open like mouths for an eternal gasp and sigh? Where among all those lovely chiseled nightmares cut from the gall-stones of night-lurks and monsters cracked out of old earthquakes, vomited up from mad vol-canoes which cooled themselves to frights and deliriums?

"Here," wailed a far, small, familiar voice again.

And way down on a ledge, halfway to the earth, the boys, squinting, thought they saw one small round beautiful angel-devil face with a familiar eye, a familiar nose, a friendly and fa-miliar mouth.

"Pipkin!"

Shouting, they ran down stairways along dark corridors until they reached a ledge. Far out there on the windy air, above a very narrow walkway indeed, was that small face, lovely among so much ugliness.

Tom went first, not looking down, spread-eagling himself. Ralph followed. The rest inched along in a line.

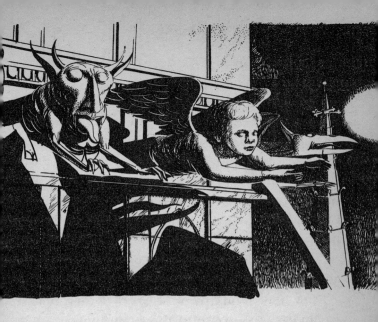

"Watch out, Tom, don't fall!"

"I'm not fallin'. Here's Pip."

And there he was.

Standing in a line directly under the out-
thrust stone mask, the bust, the head of a gargoyle, they looked up at that mighty fine profile,
that great nub nose, that unbearded cheek, that
fuzzy cap of marbled hair.

Pipkin.

"Pip, for cri-yi, what you doin' here?" called
Tom.

Pip said nothing.

His mouth was cut stone.

"Aw it's just rock," said Ralph. "Just a gargoyle carved here a long time ago, *looks* like Pipkin."

"No, I heard him *call*."

"But, how—"

And then the wind gave them the answer.

It blew around the high corners of Notre Dame. It fluted in the ears and piped out the gaping mouths of the gargoyles.

"Ahhh—" whispered Pipkin's voice.

The hair stood up on the backs of their necks.

"Ooooo," murmured the stone mouth.

"Listen. There it is!" said Ralph excitedly.

"Shut up!" cried Tom. "Pip? Next time the wind blows, tell us, how do we help? What *got* you here? How do we get you down?"

Silence. The boys clung to the rock-cliff face of the great cathedral.

Then another swoop of wind sucked by, drew their breaths, and whistled in the carved stone boy's teeth.

"One—" said Pip's voice.

"—question," whispered Pip's voice again after a pause.

Silence. More wind.

"At a—"

The boys waited.

"—time."

"One question at a time!" translated Tom.

The boys hooted with laughter. That was Pip all right.

"Okay." Tom gathered his spit. "What are you *doing* up here?"

The wind blew sadly and the voice spoke as from deep in an old well:

"Been — so many — places — in just — a few — hours."

The boys waited, grinding their teeth.

"Speak up, Pipkin!"

The wind came back to mourn in the open stone mouth:

But the wind had died.

It began to rain.

And this was best of all. For the raindrops ran cold in Pipkin's stone ears and out along his nose and fountained from his marble mouth so that he began to utter syllables in liquid tongues, with clear cold rainwater words:

"Hey—this is better!"

He spouted mist, he sprayed quick rain:

"You should've been where I been! Gosh! I was buried for a mummy! I was trapped in a dog!"

"We guessed that was you, Pipkin!"

"And now here," said the rain in the ear, the rain in the nose, the rain in the clear-dripping marble mouth. "Gosh, golly, funny, strange, inside this rock with all these devils and demons for pals! And, ten minutes from now, who knows where I'll be? higher up? or buried deep!"

"Where, Pipkin?"

The boys jostled. The rain squalled and beat them so they almost tilted and fell off the ledge.

"Are you dead, Pipkin?"

"No, not yet," said the cold rain in his mouth. "Part of me in a hospital a long way off home, part of me in that old Egyptian tomb. Part of me in the grass in England. Part of me here. Part of me in a worse place—"

"Where?"

"I don't know, I don't, oh gosh, one minute I'm yelling laughs, the next I'm scared. Now, just now, this very minute, I guess, I know, I'm scared. Help me, guys. Help, oh *please!*"

Rain poured out his eyes like tears.

130

The boys reached up to touch Pipkin's chin, as best they could. But before they could touch . . .

A lightning bolt struck out of the sky.

It flashed blue and white.

The entire cathedral shook. The boys had to grab demons' horns and angels' wings on either side so as not to be knocked off.

Thunder and smoke. And a great scattering of rock and stone.

Pipkin's face was gone. Knocked off by the lightning bolt, it fell down through space to shatter the ground below.

"Pipkin!"

But there below on the cathedral porch stones were only flinty firesparks blowing away, and a fine gargoyle dust. Nose, chin, stone lip, hard cheek, bright eye, carved fine ear, all, all whipped away on the wind in chaff and shrapnel dust. They saw something like a spirit smoke, a bloom of gunpowder blow drifting south and west.

"Mexico—" Moundshroud, one of the few men in all the world who knew how to utter, uttered the word.

"Mexico?" asked Tom.

"The last grand travel of this night," said Moundshroud, still uttering, savoring the syllables. "Whistle, boys, scream like tigers, cry like panthers, shriek like carnivore!"

"Scream, cry, shriek?"

"Reassemble the Kite, lads, the Kite of Autumn. Paste back the fangs and fiery eyes and bloody talons. Yell the wind to sew it all together and ride us high and long and last. Bray, boys, whimper, trumpet, shout!"

The boys hesitated. Moundshroud ran along the ledge like someone racketing a picket fence. He knocked each boy with his knee and elbow. The boys fell, and falling gave each his particular whimper, shriek, or scream.

Plummeting down through cold space, they felt the tail of a murderous peacock flourish beneath, all blood-filled eye. Ten thousand burning eyes came up.

Hovered suddenly round a windy corner of gargoyles, the Autumn Kite, freshly assembled, broke their fall.

They grabbed, they held to rim, to edge, to cross-struts, to trapdrum rattling papers, to bits and tatters and shreds of old meat-breath lion-mouth, and stale-blood tiger's maw.

Moundshroud leaped up to grab. This time he was the tail.

The Autumn Kite hovered, waiting, eight boys upon its billowing surf of teeth and eyes.

Moundshroud tuned his ear.

Hundreds of miles away, beggars ran down Irish roads, starving, asking for food from door to door. Their cries rose in the night.

Fred Fryer, in his beggar's costume, heard.

"That way! Let's fly there!"

"No. No time. Listen!"

Thousands of miles away, there was a faint tap-hammering of deathwatch beetles ticking the night.

"The coffin makers of Mexico." Moundshroud smiled. "In the streets with their long boxes and nails and little hammers, tapping, tapping."

"Pipkin?" whispered the boys.

"We hear," said Moundshroud. "And, to Mexico, we *go*."

The Autumn Kite boomed them away on a one-thousand-foot tidal wave of wind.

The gargoyles, fluting in their stone nostrils, gaping their marble lips, used that same wind to wail them farewell.

133

Chapter 18

They hung above Mexico.

They hung above an island in that lake in Mexico.

They heard dogs barking in the night far below. They saw a few boats on the moonlit lake moving like water insects. They heard a guitar playing and a man singing in a high sad voice.

A long way off across the dark borders of land, in the United States, packs of children, mobs of dogs ran laughing, barking, knocking, from door to door, their hands full of sweet bags of treasure, wild with joy on Halloween night.

"But, here—" whispered Tom.

"Here what?" asked Moundshroud, hovering at his elbow.

"Oh, why here—"

"And down through all of South America—"

"Yes, South. Here and South. All the cemeteries. All the graveyards are—"

—full of candlelight, Tom thought. A thousand candles in this cemetery, a hundred candles in that graveyard, ten thousand small flickering lights farther on a hundred miles, five thousand miles down to the very tip of Argentina.

"Is that the way they celebrate—"

"*El Dia de los Muertos.* How's your grade school Spanish, Tom?"

"The Day of the Dead Ones?"

"*Caramba, si!* Kite, disassemble!"

Swooping down, the Kite flew apart for a final time.

The boys tumbled on the stony shore of the quiet lake.

Mists hung over the waters.

Far across the lake they could see an unlit tombyard. There were, as yet, no candles burning in it.

Out of the mists, a dugout canoe moved silently without oars, as if the tide touched it across the waters.

A tall figure in a gray winding sheet stood motionless in one end of the boat.

The boat nudged the grassy shore softly.

The boys gasped. For, as far as they could tell,

only darkness was cupped inside the hood of the shrouded figure.

"Mr.—Mr. Moundshroud?"

They knew it had to be him.

But he said nothing. Only the faintest firefly of a grin flickered within the cowl. A bony hand gestured.

The boys tumbled into the boat.

"Sh!" whispered a voice from the empty hood.

The figure gestured again and, touched by wind, they blew across the dark waters under a night sky filled with the billion never-before-seen fires of the stars.

Far off on that dark island, there was a prickle of guitar sound.

A single candle was lit in the graveyard.

Somewhere someone blew a musical sound on a flute.

Another candle was lit among the tomb-stones.

Someone sang a single word of a song.

A third candle was touched to life by a flaming match.

And the faster the boat moved, the more guitar notes sounded and the more candles were lit high among the mounds on the stony hills. A dozen, a hundred, a thousand candles flared until it looked as if the great Andromeda star cluster had fallen out of the sky and tilted itself to rest here in the middle of almost-midnight Mexico.

The boat struck the shore. The boys, surprised, fell out. They spun about, but Moundshroud was gone. Only his winding sheet lay empty in the boat.

A guitar called to them. A voice sang to them.

A road like a river of white stones and white rocks led up through the town that was like a graveyard, to the graveyard that was like—a *town!*

For there were no people in the town.

The boys reached the low wall of the graveyard and then the huge lacework iron gates. They took hold of the iron rungs and stared in.

"Why," gasped Tom. "I never ever seen the like!"

For now they knew why the town was empty.

Because the graveyard was full.

By every grave was a woman kneeling to place gardenias or azaleas or marigolds in a frame upon the stone.

By every grave knelt a daughter who was lighting a new candle or lighting a candle that had just blown out.

By every grave was a quiet boy with bright brown eyes, and in one hand a small papier-mâché funeral parade glued to a shingle, and in the other hand a papier-mâché skeleton head which rattled with rice or nuts inside.

"Look," whispered Tom.

There were hundreds of graves. There were hundreds of women. There were hundreds of daughters. There were hundreds of sons. And hundreds upon hundreds upon thousands of candles. The whole graveyard was one swarm of candleshine as if a population of fireflies had heard of a Grand Conglomeration and had flown here to settle in and flame upon the stones and light the brown faces and the dark eyes and the black hair.

"Boy," said Tom, half to himself, "at home we never go to the graveyard, except maybe Memorial Day, once a year, and then at high noon, full sun, no fun. This now, this is—*fun!*"

"Sure!" whisper-yelled everyone.

"Mexican Halloweens are better than ours!"

For on every grave were plates of cookies shaped like funeral priests or skeletons or ghosts, waiting to be nibbled by—living people? or by ghosts that might come along toward dawn,

139

hungry and forlorn? No one knew. No one said.

And each boy inside the graveyard, next to his sister and mother, put down the miniature funeral on the grave. And they could see the tiny candy person inside the tiny wooden coffin placed before a tiny altar with tiny candles. And around the tiny coffin stood tiny altar boys with peanuts for heads and eyes painted on the peanut shells. And before the altar stood a priest with a cornnut for a head and a walnut for a stomach. And on the altar was a photograph of the person in the coffin, a real person once; remembered now.

"Better, and still better," whispered Ralph.

"*Cuevos!*" sang a far voice up the hill.

Inside the graveyard, voices echoed the song.

Leaning against the graveyard walls, some with guitars in their hands or bottles, were the men of the village.

"*Cuevos de los Muertos—*" sang the faraway voice.

"*Cuevos de los Muertos,*" sang the men in the shadows inside the gate.

"Skulls," translated Tom. "The skulls of the dead."

"Skulls, sweet sugar skulls, sweet candy skulls,

the skulls of the dead ones," sang the voice, coming close now.

And down the hill, treading softly in shadow, came a hunch-backed Vendor of Skulls.

"No, not hunched—" said Tom, half aloud.

"A whole load of *skulls* on his back," cried Ralph.

"Sweet skulls, sweet white crystal sugar candy skulls," sang the Vendor, his face hidden under a vast sombrero. But it was Moundshroud's voice that sweetly piped.

And carried from a long bamboo over his shoulder hung on black threads were dozens and scores of sugar skulls as big as their own heads. And each skull was inscribed.

"Names! Names!" sang the old Vendor. "Tell me your name, I give you your skull!"

"Tom," said Tom.

The old man plucked forth a skull. On it, in huge letters was written:

TOM.

Tom took and held his own name, his own sweet edible skull, in his fingers.

"Ralph."

And a skull with the name RALPH written on it was tossed forth. Ralph caught it, laughing.

In a swift game, the bony hand plucked, tossed white skull after skull, sweetly on the cool air:

HENRY-HANK! FRED! GEORGE! HACKLES! J.J.! WALLY!

The boys, bombarded, squealed and danced about, pelted with their own skulls and their own proud names sugar encrusted upon each white brow of those skulls. They caught and almost dropped this splendid bombardment.

They stood, mouths wide open, staring at the sugary death-sweets in their gummy hands.

And from within the graveyard, way-high male-soprano voices sang:

"Roberto . . . Maria . . . Conchita . . . Tomás.
Calavera, Calavera, *sweet candy bones to eat!*
Your name on the snow white sweet skull
You hurry down the street.
You buy from the piled high white
Hills in the square. Buy and eat!
Chew your name! What a treat!"

The boys lifted the sweet skulls in their fingers.

"Bite the T *and the* O *and the* M. Tom!
Chew the H, *Swallow* A, *Digest* N, *Choke
on* K.
Hank!"

Their mouths watered. But *was* it Poison
they held?

*"Would you guess? Such happiness, such joy
As each boy dines on darkness, makes a meal
of the night?
What delight! Snap a bite!
Go ahead! Munch that fine candy head!"*

The boys tapped the sweet candy names to
their lips and were about to bite when—
"Olé!"
A mob of Mexican boys ran up yelling their
names, seizing at skulls.
"Tomás!"
And Tom saw Tomás run off with his named
skull.
"Hey," said Tom. "He sorta looked like—
me!"
"Did he?" said the Vendor of Skulls.

143

"Enrique!" shouted a small Indian boy seizing Henry-Hank's skull.

Enrique pelted down the hill.

"He looked like *me!*" said Henry-Hank.

"He *did*," said Moundshroud. "Quick, boys, see what they're up to. Hold on to your sweet craniums and *get!*"

The boys jumped.

For at that very moment an explosion hit the streets below, in the town. Then another explosion and another. Fireworks.

The boys took a last look in at the flowers, the graves, cookies, foods, skulls upon graves, miniature funerals with miniature bodies and coffins, at candles, crouched women, lonely boys, girls, men, then whirled and exploded down the hill toward the firecrackers.

Into the plaza Tom and Ralph and all the other costumed boys raced panting. They jolted to a halt and danced about as a thousand miniature firecrackers banged around their shoes. The lights were on. Suddenly the shops were open.

And Tomás and José Juan and Enrique were lighting and tossing the firecrackers with yells.

"Hey, Tom, from *me,* Tomás!"

Tom saw his own eyes glinting from the wild boy's face.

"Hey, Henry, this from Enrique! Bang!

"J.J., this—Bang! From José Juan!"

"Oh, this is the best Halloween of all!" said Tom.

And it was.

For never in all their wild travels had so much happened to be seen, smelled, touched.

In every alley and door and window were mounds of sugar skulls with beautiful names.

From every alley came the tap-tap of death-watch-beetle coffin makers nailing, hammering, tapping coffin lids like wooden drums in the night.

On every corner were stacks of newspapers with pictures of the Mayor and his body painted in like a skeleton, or the President and his body all bones, or the loveliest maiden dressed like a xylophone and Death playing a tune on her musical ribs.

"*Calavera, Calavera, Calavera*—" the song drifted down the hill. "See the politicians buried in the news. REST IN PEACE beneath their names. Such is fame!

*"See the skeletons juggling, standing high
On each other's shoulders!
Preaching sermons, wrestling, playing soccer!
Little runners, little jumpers,
Little skeletons that leap about and fall.
Did you ever dream that death could be
Whittled down so very small?"*

And the song was true. Wherever the boys looked were the miniature acrobats, trapeze performers, basketball players, priests, jugglers, tumblers, but all were skeletons hand to hand, bony shoulder to shoulder, and all small enough for you to carry in your fingers.

And over there in a window was a whole microscopic jazz band with a skeleton trumpeter and a skeleton drummer and a skeleton playing a tuba no bigger than a soup spoon and a skeleton conductor with a bright cap on his head and a baton in his hand, and tiny music pouring out of the tiny horns.

Never before had the boys seen so many— bones!

"Bones!" laughed everyone. "Oh, *lovely* bones!"

The song began to fade:

"Hold the dark holiday in your palms,
Bite it, swallow it and survive,
Come out the far black tunnel of El Dia
    de Muerte
And be glad, ah so glad you are . . . alive!
Calavera . . . Calavera . . ."

The newspapers, bordered in black, blew away in white funerals on the wind.

The Mexican boys ran away up the hill to their families.

"Oh, strange funny strange," whispered Tom.

"What?" said Ralph at his elbow.

"Up in Illinois, we've forgotten what it's all about. I mean the dead, up in our town, tonight, heck, they're forgotten. Nobody remembers. Nobody cares. Nobody goes to sit and talk to them. Boy, that's lonely. That's really sad. But here—why, shucks. It's both happy and sad. It's all firecrackers and skeleton toys down here in the plaza and up in that graveyard now are all the Mexican dead folks with the families visiting and flowers and candles and singing and candy. I mean it's almost like Thanksgiving, huh? And everyone set down to dinner, but only half the people able to eat, but that's no

147

mind, they're *there*. It's like holding hands at a séance with your friends, but some of the friends gone. Oh, heck, Ralph."

"Yeah," said Ralph, nodding behind his mask. "Heck."

"Look, oh, look, look there," said J.J.

The boys looked.

On top of a mound of white sugar skulls was one with the name PIPKIN on it.

Pipkin's sweet skull, but—nowhere in all the explosions and dancing bones and flying skulls was there so much as one dust-speck or whimper or shadow of Pip.

They had grown so accustomed to Pip's leaping up in fantastic surprises, on the sides of Notre Dame, or weighted down in gold sarcophagi, that they had expected him, like a jack-in-the-box, to pop from a mound of sugar skulls, flap sheets in their faces, cry dirges.

But no. Suddenly, no Pip. No Pip at all.

And maybe no Pip ever again.

The boys shivered. A cold wind blew fog up from the lake.

Chapter 19

Along the dark night street, around a corner, came a woman bearing over her shoulders twin scoops of mounded charcoals, burning. From these heaps of pink burning coals firefly sparks scattered and blew in the wind. Where she passed on bare feet she left a trail of little sparks which died. Without a word, shuffling, she went around another corner into an alley, gone.

After her came a man carrying, on his head, lightly, lightly, a small coffin.

It was a box made of plain white wood nailed shut. On the sides and top of the box were pinned cheap silver rosettes, handmade silk and paper flowers.

Inside the box was—

The boys stared as the funeral parade of two went by. Two, thought Tom. The man and the box, yes, and the thing inside the box.

The man, his face solemn, balancing the coffin on the top of his head, walked tall into the nearby church.

"Was—" stuttered Tom. "Was that Pip again, inside that box?"

"What do you think, lad?" asked Mound-shroud.

"I don't know," cried Tom. "I only know I had enough. The night's been too long. I seen too much. I know everything, gosh, every-thing!"

"Yeah!" said everyone, clustering close, shiv-ering.

"And we've got to get home, don't we? What about Pipkin, where is he? Is he alive or dead? Can we save him? Is he lost? Are we too late? What do we do?"

"What!" cried everyone, and the same ques-tions flew and burst from their mouths and welled in their eyes. They all took hold of Moundshroud as if to press the answer from him, yank it out his elbows.

"What do we do?"

"To save Pipkin? One last thing. Look up in this tree!"

Dangling from the tree were a dozen Halloween piñatas: devils, ghosts, skulls, witches that swayed in the wind.

"Break your piñata, boys!"

Sticks were thrust in their hands.

"Strike!"

Yelling, they struck. The piñatas exploded.

And from the Skeleton piñata a thousand small skeleton leaves fell in a shower. They swarmed on Tom. The wind blew skeletons, leaves, and Tom away.

And from the Mummy piñata fell hundreds of frail Egyptian mummies which rushed away into the sky, Ralph with them.

And so each boy struck, and cracked and let down small vinegar-gnat dancing images of himself so that devils, witches, ghosts shrieked and seized and all the boys and leaves went tumbling through the sky, with Moundshroud laughing after.

They richocheted in the final alleys of the town. They banged and skipped like stones across the lake waters—

—to land rolling in a jumble of knees and elbows on a yet farther hill. They sat up.

They found themselves in the middle of an abandoned graveyard with no people, no lights. Only stones like immense wedding cakes, frosted with old moonlight.

And as they watched, Moundshroud, landing light on his feet in a swift quiet motion, bent. He reached for an iron rung in the earth. He pulled. With a shriek of hinges, a trapdoor in the earth gaped wide.

The boys came to stand at the edge of the big hole.

"Cat—" stuttered Tom. "Catacombs?"

"Catacombs." Moundshroud pointed.

Stairs led down into a dry dust earth.

The boys swallowed hard.

"Is Pip down there?"

"Go bring him up, boys."

"Is he *alone* down there?"

"No. Things are with him. *Things.*"

"Who goes first?"

"Not me!"

Silence.

"Me," said Tom, at last.

153

He put his foot on the first step down. He sank into the earth. He took another step. Then, suddenly, he was gone.

The others followed.

They went down the steps in single file and with each step down the dark got darker and with each step down the silence grew more silent and with each step down the night became deep as a well and very black indeed and with each step down the shadows waited and seemed to lean from walls and with each step down strange things seemed to smile at them from the long cave which waited below. Bats seemed to be hanging clustered just over their heads, squeaking so high you could not hear them. Only dogs might hear, have hysterics, jump out of their skins, and run off. With each step down the town got farther away and the earth and all the nice people of the earth. Even the graveyard above seemed far away. They felt lonely. They felt so alone they wanted to cry.

For each step down was a billion miles lost from life and warm beds and good candlelight and mothers' voices and fathers' pipe-smoke and clearing his voice in the night which made you feel good knowing he was there somewhere in the dark, alive and turning in his sleep and

154

able to hit anything with his fists if it had to be hit.

Each step down, and at last, at the bottom of the stairs, they peered into the long cave, the long hall.

And all the *people* were there and very quiet.

They had been quiet for a long time.

Some of them had been quiet for thirty years.

Some had been silent for forty years.

Some had been completely mum for seventy years.

"There they are," said Tom.

"The mummies?" someone whispered.

"The mummies."

A long line of them, standing against the walls. Fifty mummies standing against the right wall. Fifty mummies standing against the left wall. And four mummies waiting at the far end in the dark. One hundred and four dry-as-dust mummies more alone than they, more lonely than they might ever feel in life, abandoned here, left below, far from dog barks and fireflies and the sweet singing of men and guitars in the night.

"Oh, boy," said Tom. "All those poor people. I *heard* of them."

"What?"

"Their folks couldn't pay the rent on their graves, so the gravedigger dug up these people and put them down here. The earth is so dry it makes mummies out of them. And look, see how they're dressed."

The boys looked and saw that some of the ancient people were dressed like farmers and some like peasant maids and some like businessmen in old dark suits, and one even like a bullfighter in his dusty suit of lights. But inside their suits they were all thin bones and skin and spiderweb and dust that shook down through their ribs if you sneezed and trembled them.

"What's that?"

"What, what?"

"Ssssst!"

Everyone listened.

They peered into the long vault.

All the mummies looked back with empty eyes. All the mummies waited with empty hands.

Someone was weeping at the far end of the long dark hall.

"Ahhh—" came the sound.

"Oh—" came the crying.

156

"eeee—" and the small voice wept.

"That's—why, that's Pip. Only heard him cry once, but that's him. Pipkin. And he's trapped there in the catacomb."

The boys stared.

And they saw, a hundred feet away, crouched down in a corner, trapped at the most distant part of the catacomb, a small figure that—moved. The shoulders twitched. The head was bent and covered with trembling hands. And behind the hands, the mouth wailed and was afraid.

"Pipkin—?"

The crying stopped.

"Is that *you?*" whispered Tom.

A long pause, a trembled insuck of breath and then:

". . . yes."

"Pip, for cri-yi, what you doing there?"

"I don't know!"

"Come out?"

"I—I can't. I'm afraid!"

"But, Pip, if you stay there—"

Tom paused.

Pip, he thought, if you stay, you stay forever. You stay with all the silence and the lonely ones.

157

Ray Bradbury

You stand in the long line and tourists come and look at you and buy tickets to look at you some more. You—

"Pip!" said Ralph behind his mask. "You got to come out."

"I can't." Pip sobbed. "*They* won't let me."

"They?"

But they knew he meant the long line of mummies. In order to get out he would have to run the gauntlet between the nightmares, the mysteries, the dreadful ones, the dires and the haunts.

"*They* can't stop you, Pip."

Pip said: "Oh, yes, they can."

". . . can . . ." said echoes deep in the catacomb.

"I'm afraid to come out."

"And we're—" said Ralph.

Afraid to go in, thought everyone.

"Maybe if we chose *one* brave one—" said Tom, and stopped.

For Pipkin was crying again, and the mummies waiting and the night so dark in the long tomb hall that you would sink right through the floor if you stepped on it, and never move again. The floor would seize your ankles with

158

bony marble and hold you until the freezing cold froze you into a dry-dust statue forever.

"Maybe if we went in in a mob, all of us—" said Ralph.

And they tried to move.

Like a big spider with many legs, the boys tried to cram through the door. Two steps forward, one step back. One step forward, two steps back.

"Ahhhhh!" wept Pipkin.

At which sound they all fell upon themselves, gibbering, and scrambled yelling their dires and frights back to the door. They heard an avalanche of heartbeats bang pains in their chests.

"Oh, my gosh, what we gonna do, him afraid to come, us afraid to go, what, what?" wailed Tom.

Behind them, leaning against the wall, was Moundshroud, forgotten. A little candleflame of smile flickered and went out among his teeth.

"Here, boys. Save him with *this.*"

Moundshroud reached into his dark cloak and brought forth a familiar white-sugar-candy skull across the brow of which was written:

159

PIPKIN!

"Save Pipkin, lads. Strike a bargain."

"With who?"

"With me and others unnamed. Here. Break this skull in eight delicious bits, boys, hand them 'round. *P* for you, Tom, and *I* for you, Ralph, and half of the other *P* for you, Hank, the other half for you, J.J., and some of the *K* for you, boy, and some for you, and here's the *I* and the final *N*. Touch the sweet bits, lads. Listen. Here's the dark deal. Do you truly want Pipkin to live?"

Such a fury of protest burst forth at this, Moundshroud was fair driven back by it. The boys barked like dogs against his so much as questioning their need for Pip's survival.

"There, there," he curried them, "I see you mean it. Well then, will you each give one year from the end of your life, boys?"

"What?" said Tom.

"I mean it, boys, one year, one precious year from the far-burned candle-end of your life. With one year apiece you can ransom dead Pipkin."

"A year!" the whisper, the murmur, the appalling sum of it ran among them. It was hard to grasp. A year so far away was no year at all. Boys of eleven or twelve cannot guess at men of seventy. "A year? a year? why, sure, why not? Yes—"

"Think, boys, think! This is no idle bargain struck with Nothing. I mean it. It is true and a fact. It is a grave condition you make, and a grave bargain you strike.

"One year, each of you must promise to give. You won't miss the year now, of course, for you are very young, and I see by touching your minds you cannot even guess the final situation. Only later, fifty years from this night, or sixty years from this dawn, when you are running low on time and dearly wish an extra day or so of fine weather and much joy, then's when Mr. D for Doom or Mr. B for Bones will show up with his bill to be paid. Or perhaps I will come, old Moundshroud himself, a friend to lads, and say 'deliver.' So a year promised must be a year given over. I'll say 'give,' and you must give.

"What will that mean to each of you?

"It will mean that those of you who might have lived to be seventy-one must die at seventy. Some of you who might have lived to be eighty-six must cough up your ghost at eighty-five.

That's a great age. A year more or less doesn't sound like much. When the time comes, boys, you may regret. But, you will be able to say, *this* year I spent well, I gave for Pip, I made a loan of life for sweet Pipkin, the fairest apple that ever almost fell too early off the harvest tree. Some of you at forty-nine must cross life off at forty-eight. Some at fifty-five must lay them down to Forever's Sleep at fifty-four. Do you catch the whole thing intact now, boys? Do you add the figures? Is the arithmetic plain? A year! Who will bid three hundred and sixty-five entire days from out his own soul, to get old Pipkin back? Think, boys. Silence. Then, speak."

There was a long brooding silence of arithmetic students doing inward sums.

And the sums were very fast indeed. There was no question, though they knew that years from now they might doubt this dreadful haste. Yet what else could they do? Only swim out from shore and save the drowning boy before he sank a last time into a frightening dust.

"Me," said Tom. "I'll give a year."

"And me," said Ralph.

"I'm in," said Henry-Hank.

And, "Me!" "Me!" "Me!" said all the rest.

"Do you know what you pledge, boys? You *do* love Pipkin, then?"

"Yes, *yes!*"

"So be it, boys. Chew and eat, lads, eat and chew."

They popped the sweet bits of candy skull in their mouths.

They chewed. They ate.

"Swallow darkness, boys, give up your year."

They swallowed hard, so hard that their eyes shone bright and their ears banged and their hearts beat.

They felt something like a cage of birds let out of their chests and bodies and flying off, invisible. They saw but did not see the years they gave as gifts wing off round the world to settle somewhere in good payment for strange debts.

They heard a yell.

"Here!"

And then: "I!"

And then: "Come!"

Bang, bang, bang, the three words, and three sounds of shoes hitting stone.

And along the hall and between the rows of

mummies which leaned out to stop but did not
stop, between the silent shrieks and screams,
hellbent, rushing, racing, flinging his feet,
pumping his elbows, puffing his cheeks, shutting his eyes, snorting his nostrils, and bang
bang banging the floor with his up and down,
up and down feet, came—

Pipkin.

Oh how he *ran!!!*

"Look at him come. Come on, Pip."

"Pip, you're halfway!"

"Look at him race!" said everyone with sugar
candy in their mouths, with the honorable name
of Pipkin locked in their sweet teeth, with his
savor in their jaws, with his fine name on their
tongues, Pip, Pip, Pipkin!

"Don't stop now, Pip. Don't look *back!*"

"Don't fall down!"

"Here he comes, three quarters of the way!"

Pip ran the gauntlet. He was good and fine
and fast and true. Between one hundred waiting
mummies he ran without touching and did not
look back and—won the race.

"Pip, you did it!"

"You're safe!"

But Pip kept running. Not only through the

gauntlet of dead ones but the gauntlet of warm sweating alive yelling boys.

He plowed then aside and raced upstairs, gone.

"Pip, it's all right, come back!"

They ran up the stairs after.

"Where's he going, Mr. Moundshroud?"

"Well, I should imagine, scared as he is," said Moundshroud, "home."

"Is Pipkin—saved?"

"Let's go see, boys. Up!"

He spun about like a whirlwind. His arms, flung out, cut the air in slicing grabs and swoops. So fast he spun that he made a vacuum, a self-made storm. This cyclone, this huge upsuck of air, then seized the boys by ear, nose, elbow, toe.

Like so many leaves stripped from a tree they yelled themselves into the sky. Moundshroud, raving, sank up. And they, if that is possible, sank and plummeted after. They hit the clouds like an explosion of gunshot. They followed Moundshroud like a flock of north-rushing birds heading home before their season.

The earth seemed to give a turn from north to south. A thousand small villages and towns spun under, alight with candles flickering in

165

tombyards through all of Mexico, alight with candles flickering in pumpkins north of the border across Texas and then Oklahoma and Kansas and Iowa and at last Illinois and at last:

"Home!" cried Tom. "There's the court-house, there's *my* house, there's the Halloween Tree!"

They swooped once around the courthouse and twice around the thousand-pumpkin-burn-ing Tree, and a final time around old Mound-shroud's tall house with its many gables, many rooms, many gaping windows, high lightning rods, railings, attics, scrollworks, which leaned and groaned in the wind their passage made. Dust sifted out of windows to greet them. Shades flapped in yet other windows like ancient tongues lolling to be diagnosed by wind-borne small doctors of strange medicines. Ghosts with-ered like white flowers, furling and unfurling in moldered flags which fell to ruin even as they shot by.

And the whole house, circled, was like all of Halloween ever. So cried Moundshroud, flap-ping his antique arms and webs and black silks as he landed on the roof and beckoned the boys to alight and pointed down through an immense sky window through all the levels of his mansion.

The boys gathered round the skylight window and stared down a stairwell which opened out at various floors to various times and histories of men and skeletons and dreadful musics played on flute bones.

"There it is, boys. Will you look? Do you see? There's our whole ten-thousand-year flight, there's our whole trip in one place, from caveman to Egyptian to Roman front porch to English harvest field to boneyard in Mexico."

Moundshroud lifted the vast pane of glass.

"The stairway banister, boys. Ride it down! Each to his own time, his own age, his own level. Leap off where your costume fits, where you think you and your disguise, your mask, belong! Git!"

The boys leaped. They sprang down the stairwell to the top landing. Then, one by one, they popped onto the banister and slid yelling down through all the floors, all the levels, all the ages of history kept within Moundshroud's incredible mansion.

167

Round-about-down, round-about-down they whisked, they skidded, they shuffled on the waxed rail.

Rrrwhoom-thud! J.J. in his Apeman costume landed in the basement. He glanced about. He saw cave paintings, dim smokes and fires, and shadows of hulking gorilla-men. Saber-tooths burned their eyes at him from the cindered dark.

Down-around rush went Ralph, the Egyptian Mummified Boy, bandaged for all ages, to land on the first floor where Egyptian hieroglyphs strutted in armies of symbol, with squadrons of ancient birds in skies and flocks of beast-gods and scuttling golden beetles rolling dung-balls down history.

Crash! Hackles Nibley, with his scythe somehow still flashing in his hands, hit and almost rolled himself to mincemeat on the second floor where the shadow of Samhain, druid God of the Dead, raised up his scythe upon a far chamber wall!

Bang! George Smith, a Greek Ghost? a Roman Haunt? landed on the third floor near tarpainted porches which glued old wandering spirits to the sill!

Thud, Henry-Hank, the Witch, plopped

down in the fourth landing amid witches leaping bonfires in English, French, German countrysides!

Fred Fryer? The fifth floor took him in a heap, the Beggar landing among sounds of beggars begging the country roads of Ireland, starving.

Wally Babb, the Gargoyle himself, flew and crashed on the sixth floor where walls sprouted elbows and limbs and lumps, grimaces of fine gargoyle humors and glees.

Until finally Skeleton Tom skidded off the banister on the topmost floor to tumble and knock white candy skulls like tenpins in a dire game among the shadows of crouched women by mounds, with miniature skeleton brassbands playing mosquito tunes while Moundshroud, far above, still on the roof, yelled down:

"Well, boys, do you *see?* It's all one, yes?"

"Yes—" someone murmured.

"Always the same but different, eh? every age, every time. Day was always over. Night was always coming. And aren't you always afraid, Apeman there? or you, Mummy, that the sun will never rise again?"

"Yesss," more of them whispered.

And they looked up through the levels of the

169

great house and saw every age, every story, and all the men in history staring round about as the sun rose and set. Apemen trembled. Egyptians cried laments. Greeks and Romans paraded their dead. Summer fell dead. Winter put it in the grave. A billion voices wept. The wind of time shook the vast house. The windows rattled and broke like men's eyes, into crystal tears. Then, with cries of delight, ten thousand times a million men welcomed back bright summer suns which rose to burn each window with fire!

"Do you see, lads? Think! People vanished forever. They died, oh Lord, they died! but came back in dreams. Those dreams were called Ghosts, and frightened men in every age—"

"Ah!" cried a billion voices from attics and basements.

Shadows climbed walls like old films rerun in ancient theaters. Puffs of smoke lingered at doors with sad eyes and gibbering mouths.

"Night and day. Summer and winter, boys. Seedtime and harvest. Life and death. That's what Halloween is, all rolled up in one. Noon and midnight. Being born, boys. Rolling over, playing dead like dogs, lads. And getting up again, barking, racing through thousands of years of death each day and each night Hallow-een, boys, every night, every single night dark and fearful until at last you made it and hid in cities and towns and had some rest and could get your breath.

"And you began to live longer and have more time, and space out the deaths, and put away fear, and at last have only special days in each year when you thought of night and dawn and spring and autumn and being born and being dead.

"And it all adds up. Four thousand years ago, one hundred years ago, this year, one place or another, but the celebrations all the *same*—"

"The Feast of Samhain—"

"The Time of the Dead Ones—"

"All Souls'. All Saints'."

"The Day of the Dead."

"*El Dia De Muerte*."

"All Hallows'."

"Halloween."

The boys sent their frail voices up, up through the levels of time, from all the countries, and all the ages, naming the holidays which were the same.

"Good, lads, good."

Far off, the town clock struck three quarters after eleven.

"Almost midnight, boys. Halloween's almost over."

"But!" cried Tom. "What about Pipkin? We followed him through history, burying him, digging him up, walking him in parades, crying him in wakes. Is or *isn't* he alive?"

"Yeah!" said everyone. *"Did* we save him?"

"Did you, indeed?"

Moundshroud stared. They stared with him, across the ravine to a building where lights were going out.

"That's his hospital, boys. But check his house. The final knock of the night, the last grand trick or treat. Go ask for final answers. Mr. Marley, see them *out!"*

The front door flew wide—bang!

The Marley knocker on the door gaped its bandaged jaw and whistled them farewell as the boys slid down the banisters and raced for the door.

They were stopped by a final shout from Moundshroud: "Boys! Well, which was it? Tonight, with me—trick or *treat?"*

The boys took a vast breath, held it, burst it out: "Gosh, Mr. Moundshroud—*both!*"

Rap! went the Marley knocker.

Slam! went the door.

And the boys were gone running, running down through the ravine and up along the street gasping hot gusts of air, their masks falling to be trampled until at last they stopped on Pipkin's sidewalk and looked at the far hospital and back at Pipkin's front door.

"You go, Tom, you," said Ralph.

And Tom slowly edged up to the house and put his foot on the front step and then the second step up and approached the door, afraid to knock, afraid to find the final answer about dear old Pipkin. Pipkin dead? Pipkin in a last funeral? Pipkin, Pipkin gone forever? No!

He tapped at the door.

The boys waited on the sidewalk.

The door opened. Tom went in. There was a long moment of the boys on the sidewalk standing cold and letting the wind freeze their most awful thoughts.

Well? they yelled silently in at the house, the shut door, the dark windows, well? well? What?

And then at last the door opened again, and

Tom came out and stood on the porch not knowing where he was.

Then Tom looked up and saw his friends waiting for him a million miles off.

Tom leaped off the porch, yelling.

"Oh gosh, oh gosh, oh, Gosh!"

He ran along the sidewalk, shrieking: "He's okay, he's all right, he's okay! Pipkin's in the hospital! took his appendix out at nine tonight! got it just in time! doctor says he's great!"

"Pipkin—?"

"Hospital—?"

"Great—?"

The air jumped out as if each had been punched in the stomach. Then the air went in and out again in a great rave, a yell, a ragged shout of triumph.

"Pipkin, oh, Pipkin, Pip!"

And the boys stood on Pipkin's lawn and the sidewalk in front of Pipkin's porch and house and looked with numb curiosity at each other as their smiles spread and their eyes watered and they yelled and the happy tears ran down their cheeks.

"Oh, boy, boy oh boy, oh boy oh boy," said Tom, exhausted, and weeping with happiness.

"You can say that again," said someone, and they all said it again.

And they all stood there and had a fine happy cry.

And since the whole night was turning soupy with tears, Tom looked around and revved them up. "Look at Pipkin's house. Don't it look awful? Tell you what we do—!"

And they ran and each came back carrying a lit pumpkin and lined them up on Pipkin's porch rail where they smiled outrageous smiles to wait for Pipkin to come home.

And they stood on the lawn and looked at the lovely sight of all those smiles, their costumes tattered upon their arms and shoulders and legs, and the greasepaint dripped and running on their faces, and a great wondrous happy tiredness gathering in their eyelids and arms and feet, but not wanting to go yet.

And the town clock struck midnight—GUN-NNG!

And gunnng again, to a full count of twelve.

And Halloween was over.

And all about the town, doors were slamming and lights going out.

The boys began to drift saying Night and Night and again Night and some Good Night but most Night, yes, Night. And the lawn was empty, but Pipkin's porch was just full of candle illumination and warmth and baked pumpkin smell.

And Ghost and Mummy and Skeleton and Witch and all the rest were back at their own homes, on their own porches, and each turned to look at the town and remember this special night they would never in all their lives ever forget and they looked across the town at one another's porches but especially on and over across the ravine to that great House where at the very top Mr. Moundshroud stood on his spike-railinged roof.

The boys waved, each from his own porch.

The smoke curling out of the high Moundshroud gothic chimney fluttered, motioned, waved back.

And still more doors were slamming to lock all around town.

And with each slam, one more pumpkin and then another and another and another on the huge Halloween Tree snuffed out. By the dozens, by the hundreds, by the thousands, doors banged, pumpkins went blind, snuffed candles smoked delicious smokes.

The Witch hesitated, went in, shut the door.

A Witch-faced pumpkin on the Tree went dark.

The Mummy stepped into his house and shut his door.

A pumpkin with the face of a mummy extinguished its light.

And finally, the last boy in all the town remaining alone on his veranda, Tom Skelton in his skull and bones hating to go in, wanting to wring the last dear drop from his favorite holiday in all the year, sent his thoughts on the night air toward the strange house beyond the ravine:

Mr. Moundshroud, who are YOU?

And Mr. Moundshroud, way up there on the roof, sent his thoughts back:

I think you know, boy, I think you know.

Will we meet again, Mr. Moundshroud?

Many years from now, yes, I'll come for you.

And a last thought from Tom:

O Mr. Moundshroud, will we EVER *stop being afraid of nights and death?*

And the thought returned:

When you reach the stars, boy, yes, and live there forever, all the fears will go, and Death himself will die.

Tom listened, heard, and waved quietly.

Mr. Moundshroud, far off, lifted his hand.

Click. Tom's front door went shut.

His pumpkin-like-a-skull, on the vast Tree, sneezed and went dark.

The wind stirred the great Halloween Tree which was now empty of all light save one pumpkin at the very top.

A pumpkin with Mr. Moundshroud's eyes and face.

At the top of the house, Mr. Moundshroud leaned out, took a breath, blew.

His candle in his pumpkin head on the Tree fluttered, died.

Miraculously, smoke curled out of his own mouth, his nose, his ears, his eyes, as if his soul had been extinguished within his lungs at the very moment the sweet pumpkin gave up its incensed ghost.

He sank down into his house. The roof trap-door closed.

The wind came by. It rocked all the dark

smoking pumpkins on the vast and beautiful Halloween Tree. The wind seized a thousand dark leaves and blew them away up over the sky and down over the earth toward the sun that must surely rise.

Like the town, the Tree turned off its embered smiles and slept.

At two in the morning, the wind came back for more leaves.

ABOUT THE AUTHOR

RAY BRADBURY was born in Waukegan, Illinois, in 1920. He graduated from a Los Angeles high school in 1938. His formal education ended there, but he furthered it by himself—at night in the library and by day at his typewriter. He sold newspapers on Los Angeles street corners from 1938 to 1942, a modest beginning for a man whose name would one day be synonymous with the best in science fiction. Ray Bradbury sold his first science fiction short story in 1941, and his early reputation is based on stories published in the budding science fiction magazines of that time. His work was chosen for best American short story collections in 1946, 1948 and 1952. His awards include The O. Henry Memorial Award, the Benjamin Franklin Award in 1954 and The Aviation-Space Writer's Association Award for best space article in an American magazine in 1967. Mr. Bradbury has written for television, radio, the theater and film, and he has been published in every major American magazine. Editions of his novels and shorter fiction span several continents and languages, and he has gained worldwide acceptance for his work. His titles include *The Martian Chronicles, Fahrenheit 451, Dandelion Wine, Something Wicked This Way Comes, I Sing the Body Electric, The Golden Apples of the Sun, A Medicine for Melancholy, The Illustrated Man, Long After Midnight, The Stories of Ray Bradbury, Dinosaur Tales* and *The Toynbee Convector*.

ABOUT THE ILLUSTRATOR

JOSEPH MUGNAINI is a professor of art at the Otis Art Institute. He has written two books on painting and drawing. Three of his lithographs have been placed in the permanent collection of the Library of Congress. He lives in California with his family.